EXPATS

C.J. JESSOME

© C.J. JESSOME
All rights reserved.

3369 Beach Ave.
Roberts Creek, BC
Canada
V0N2W2

DEDICATION

To the people of Puerto Morelos,

You welcomed me with open arms when I came to your town as a single expat woman. You showed me kindness, generosity, and warmth that I will never forget. You made me feel at home and part of your family. You are the reason why I fell in love with Puerto Morelos and why I will always cherish it in my heart. Thank you for being my friends, my neighbors, and my second family.

This book is dedicated to you.

Expats

CONTENTS

Dedication	iii
About the Author	vii
Synopsis	ix
Perfect Day in Paradise	1
The Betrayal	20
The Plan Begins	32
All Hands on Deck	36
Security Team Arrives	45
Brian Arrives in Sochi	54
Brian And Katya in Haifa	65
Natalie is Missing	74
The Cartel Connection	79
Brian and Katya Back in Mexico	87
Who is Natalie?	95
Nikos Confession	101
Confronting Steve Stevens	107
The Climax	115
Loose Ends	121

Expats

ABOUT THE AUTHOR

C.J. JESSOME has a unique background that informs her writing. She obtained a science degree and studied law at Dalhousie University, where she developed a keen interest in international affairs and human rights. She also had exposure to the military, having served in the Canadian Coast Guard. She later pursued her passion for creative writing, taking courses and workshops from renowned authors and mentors. She is also an artist, an entrepreneur, and an avid trader, with a flair for innovation and risk-taking. C.J. JESSOME currently divides her time between Vancouver, Canada and Puerto Morelos, Mexico.

Expats

SYNOPSIS

EXPATS
THE PUERTO MORELOS CONNECTION

Whiskey, a retired engineer from Texas, spends his winters in Puerto Morelos, Mexico, with his expat friends. They have diverse and colorful backgrounds, from spying to hacking, from journalism to Wall Street. But their peace is broken when Whiskey falls for Katya, a Russian spy who steals his classified documents. Katya's handlers need the intel to sabotage an oil pipeline. Whiskey and his friends must stop the attack from happening and expose the true actors and intentions behind the plot, in order to stop the world from falling into chaos and likely a world war. Whiskey and his team face shocking secrets, unexpected allies, and deadly enemies. EXPATS is a thrilling novel of action, intrigue, and friendship.

Expats

Chapter 1
PERFECT DAY IN PARADISE

Puerto Morelos sparkles like a hidden jewel on the Yucatan Peninsula, Mexico. For the expats who have made it their home, it is a sanctuary where they can forget about the troubles of the world....

I'm Whiskey, a Black 72-year-old retired oil pipeline engineer. Life has been one hell of a ride, and I've got four failed marriages under my belt, and a world renowned pipeline engineering company, to prove it. But now, waking up each day in my beautiful villa overlooking the Caribbean ocean, I feel like I'm able to live a simpler life.

"Another perfect day in Mexico," I muse to myself, stretching lazily in my king-sized bed.

As the first light of dawn creeps over the horizon, I rise from my bed and stretch, feeling a few creaks and groans of my body. My villa, on the Caribbean Sea, offers an unparalleled view of the sunrise, and I never miss an opportunity to savor it. The sky explodes with colors as the sun rises, casting a warm glow on the turquoise water, beckoning me. They say money can't buy happiness, but they never mentioned the feeling you get when you wake up to this every morning.

As I get ready for another day in this tropical wonderland, my thoughts drift to my expat friends. They are a diverse and lively bunch of people who have become like family to me. We have escaped the stress and troubles of our old lives, and now we enjoy the beauty and tranquility of this place.

"Time for a swim," I murmur, slipping into my bathing suit and heading down the stone steps to the beach. The sand is cool beneath my feet as I wade into the warm water, allowing the gentle waves to envelop me. With each stroke, I feel more alive. I've always loved the ocean, a passion that has only grown stronger since I purchased the Villa ten years ago as a vacation property.

After my morning swim, I make my way to El Nicho, the breakfast spot where I know it will be busy. The intoxicating aroma of fresh coffee and sizzling bacon wafts through the air as I step inside. Marco, the owner, greets me with his usual boisterous enthusiasm.

"Whiskey! You're right on time, as always!" he exclaims. "Your huevos rancheros are almost ready!"

"Thanks, Marco, I don't know what I'd do without your cooking."

"Starve, probably!" he jokes, slapping me on the back before returning to the kitchen.

"Morning, Whiskey," Ana, Marco's wife, calls out from behind the bakery counter. Her eyes sparkle with warmth, and I can see she's been working hard rolling pastry.

"Check out Karlie's new pieces on the wall," she adds, pointing to a stunning seascape in soft pastel hues, next to it, much to my surprise, is a painting of our expat crew sitting in our Tommy Bahama chairs on the beach.

"Beautiful work, Karlie has such a gift. I'll take the one of us on the beach. I'll send Pedro down for it later."

"Good morning, Whiskey," chimes in Bob from his usual spot at the corner table, nursing a steaming cup of coffee. His wife, Becca, sits across from him, engrossed in her book.

"Morning, Bob. Hi, Becca," I greet them, accepting my plate from Marco as he emerges from the kitchen. The huevos rancheros are a masterpiece of flavor, and I dig in with gusto.

How are you today?"

"We're good, Whiskey. Thanks for asking. How about you?" Bob answered, his voice warm and friendly.

"Couldn't be better," I say, gesturing to the sky.

"Yeah, it's a beautiful day. Perfect for reading a book," Becca grumbled, holding up the paperback she was reading. She is an avid reader, especially of thrillers and mysteries.

"What are you reading, Becca?"

"It's a thriller about a hacker who tries to expose a corrupt corporation."

"Sounds interesting. Is it based on a true story?"

"Well, not exactly. But it reminds me of some of the things I did when I was working in Silicon Valley," Becca says, with a hint of pride in her voice.

"Really? Like what?"

"Oh, you know. Just hacking into some systems, finding some secrets, exposing some frauds. Nothing too serious," Becca says casually.

"Nothing too serious? That sounds pretty serious to me."

"Nah, it was all in good fun. And I made a lot of money from it too. I sold my cyber security start-up to Microsoft, remember?" Becca says, reminding Whisky of her biggest accomplishment.

"How could I forget? You remind me every day," I joke, making Becca laugh.

"Don't mind her, Whisky. She's just bragging. She always does that when she reads these books," Bob says, rolling his eyes.

"And what are you up to, Bob?"

"Me? I just drink my coffee and watch the world go by," Bob says, shrugging.

"That sounds relaxing. Do you miss Silicon Valley?"

Bob smiled, his eyes twinkling with remembered pride. "Sometimes, I look back and marvel at what we did. I mean, the cloud computing platforms we created were nothing short of masterpieces!" He shook his head in awe, running a hand along the table top absently.

"Wow, that's impressive."

"Yeah, it was. But it was also stressful and exhausting. I'm glad I retired when I did."

With a satisfied sigh, I push away from the table and bid farewell to my friends. As I step outside El Nicho, the favorite part of my day begins, a walk along the beach.

"See you later, Marco, Ana!" I call out, and wave at them, seeing their friendly smiles as they wave back.

My feet move slowly on the cobblestones, feeling their uneven shapes. The Casa Walls that line the quiet streets, overflow with bougainvillea, a cascade of red and fuchsia petals. I lift my face to the sun, a blazing orb in the sky.

As I walk along the beach, I feel a sense of peace and gratitude. I've worked hard to get where I am today, and I've earned every bit of it. No one can take that away from me. Not the government, not the media, not the environmentalists, not the terrorists.

Scanning the beach I notice her – a captivating presence that stands out from the others.

The woman is walking along the shoreline, her long, black hair cascading down her back as she moves with an effortless grace. She looks like a vision straight out of a dream, and I can't help but feel a magnetic pull towards her. Even from a distance, I sense something special about her – a mysterious allure that piques my curiosity.

"Who is she?" I wonder, feeling a sudden urge to meet this enchanting stranger.

As if she can sense my gaze, she veers off her path, heading towards Dive Bar. Seeing my opportunity, I follow her down to the bar, a little more pep in my step.

I spot Josh and Karlie sitting on stools. They wave at me as I approach them, and I smile back. Josh is a former Wall Street hedge fund manager. After some trouble with the SEC he retired and spends several months of the year here. He met Karlie, a former journalist, now an aspiring artist and Canadian expat, They met at her La Sirena paint and sip class here in Puerto Morelos. Now they live, travel and go on adventures together. They are one of the youngest couples in our group, and they have a zest for life that is contagious.

"Hey, Whiskey," Josh greets me. "How's your morning?"

"Great, as always." Turning my attention to Karlie, "I saw your amazing paintings. You captured us all so well. It's fantastic! I've got the perfect spot for it!"

Karlie beams at me and gives me a hug. "Oh Whiskey, you're too kind. I'm glad you like it."

"Like it? I love it! Thank you so much."

"Hey Josh, what do you think of the painting?"

Josh grins, "I think it's great. Especially the part where Karlie gave herself bigger boobs and a smaller waist."

Karlie rolls her eyes and punches him in the arm.

"Shut up Josh! I did not do that. Then laughing she remarks, "it's called artistic licence."

"Sure, sure. Whatever you say," Josh says, rubbing his arm.

I laugh and shake my head. "You two are hilarious. So what are you up to today?"

"We just finished a game of bocce ball, I won!, Karlie beams.

"Congratulations, I hope you will be on my team for Sunday's tournament?"

"You got it, Whiskey! I need a new partner, I'm on a losing streak with this guy," Karlie says, pointing her bottle towards Josh.

"You know, speaking of trying new things, I have something to tell you."

"What is it?" Karlie asks, curious.

"I've decided to invest in a new venture."

"Really? What kind of venture?" Josh asks.

"It's a space tourism company."

"Space tourism?" Karlie repeats, incredulous.

"That's right. It's called Starbound, and it's going to offer suborbital flights to the edge of space for anyone who can afford it."

"Wow," Josh says. "That sounds amazing."

"It is, I've always wanted to go to space, ever since I was a kid. And now I have the chance to make it happen."

"That's incredible," Karlie says. "But isn't it risky? I mean, space travel is not exactly safe or easy."

"It's not without its challenges, sure," I admit. "But nothing worthwhile ever is. And besides, Starbound has some of the best engineers and pilots in the industry. They've been working on this project for years, and they've tested everything extensively. They're confident that they can deliver a safe and unforgettable experience for their customers."

"And you trust them?" Josh asks.

"I do, I've met them personally, and I've seen their work. They're smart, dedicated, and visionary. Just like me."

"And you know what? You two are invited to join me on the inaugural flight."

"Really?" Karlie gasps.

"Really."

"When is it?" Josh asks.

"Next month."

"Next month?" Karlie repeats.

"That's right."

"Wow," Josh says.

"So, what do you say? Are you in?"

They look at each other for a moment, then back at me. They smile, "We're in," they say in unison.

"Excellent, let's toast to that."

"Ola Griffin!" I shout, trying to get the bar owner's attention, who I see fiddling out back with scuba equipment.

Griffin shuffled out of the shadow, wiping his forehead with a rag. His rotund frame was barely contained by the stained tank top and Hawaiian shorts he wore. His upper lip glistened with sweat as he extended his left hand to me.

"Ah, I'm so sorry, pal. Didn't see you there," he said showing his Canadian roots. Griffin loves diving and being beneath the waves more than anything else. I'm sure buoyancy provides a big relief.

"Another round of cerveza, por favor."

He slid them across.

We take them with excitement.

I raise my bottle.

"To Starbound!"

"To Starbound!" they echo.

We clink our bottles and take a long cold swig. We gaze at the sky, laughter bubbling from us.

"Vodka on the rocks," a voice says over my shoulder, rich and alluring with a Russian accent.

Turning with a smile towards the woman I just followed up the beach. "Hey there, Vodka" I say, slipping onto the empty stool beside her. "I'm Whisky."

"Katya," she chuckles. "You use that line a lot?" Her eyes hold a knowing glint, as though she's been expecting me all along.

"Nice to meet you, Katya. What brings you to Puerto Morelos?" I ask, eager to learn more about her.

"Vacation," she answers simply, "And you?"

"Retirement, more or less. I fell in love with this place years ago but only recently been able to stay for extended periods."

"Ah, you are a local expert then," she teases, "Maybe you can show me around?"

"Absolutely," I respond, our conversation flowing effortlessly as we continue to chat over our drinks.

It's clear to me that Katya is very sharp. She knows just how to keep me engaged and interested, and I find myself falling under the spell of this much younger beauty.

"Here's to new friends and new adventures," I toast, clinking my bottle against her glass.

"Za oospeh! which means "To success!" she says.

Her steel blue eyes locked onto mine, sending a shiver. I can't help but feel that my world has shifted – and I'm eager to see where this goes. "Have you ever been snorkeling?"

"Yes, I like to snorkel," she admits, turning to face me, "The underwater world is so magical, full of life, yet so serene.

"Then you're in for a treat," I say, feeling a surge of excitement at the prospect of exploring the nearby coral reefs together. "The reef just off the coast here is teeming with marine life. You'll love it."

"Sounds good," she replies, her eyes sparkling with anticipation. "I will go."

As the afternoon turns to evening, we find ourselves enjoying the terrace at La Sirena restaurant by the town square. Under the palapa, soft candlelight flickers across Katya's face, casting shadows that dance in harmony with the swaying palms. Our conversation flows effortlessly, weaving through topics that reveal our shared interests – the beauty of the ocean, the allure of foreign lands, and our mutual appreciation for Art, especially the Old Masters.

"Whiskey," she says, her voice barely audible over the Salsa band that began to play, "I'm glad we met. There's something about you I like."

"Katya, me too," I admit, my heart swelling with affection for this captivating woman who has so unexpectedly entered my life.

I reach out, tap her hand, feeling the warmth of her skin against mine. We've ordered some appetizers and drinks, and we're waiting for our main courses. We're chatting and getting to know each other better.

"So, Whisky, what do you do for a living?"

"Well, I'm a pipeline engineer."

"Wow, that's impressive. How did you get into that business?"

"Oh that's a long story, maybe another day," I say, feeling hopeful if not a little presumptuous.

"And you, being a Russian woman, what do you do for work?" I ask her, curious about how her culture influences her career choices.

"I'm a sailing instructor."

"Really? That sounds cold. In Russia?"

"I live near the Black Sea, which is the warmest and most popular sea for sailing in Russia."

"Where on the Black Sea?"

"Sochi. I've always loved sailing since I was a little girl. My father was a sailor too, and he taught me how to sail on his boat. He also taught me to love and respect the sea," she says fondly.

"That's wonderful. Do you have your own boat?"

"Yes, I do. It's a small but cozy sailboat that I named Katya's Dream."

"Katya's Dream? That's a nice name. Can I see it sometime?" I ask her hopefully.

"Sure, why not? Maybe we can go sailing together one day," she says flirtatiously.

"I'd love that."

We smile at each other and clink our glasses. We're having a great time together, and I feel a connection with her. Just then, the owner of the restaurant comes over to our table. He's a friendly man named Paul Pappas who greets us warmly. "Hello, Whisky. How are you enjoying your meal?" he asks us.

"Excellent so far! We are waiting on the fresh red snapper."

"This is Katya, my new friend from Russia," I say, pleased to introduce her to Paul.

"Katya, welcome," Paul says. "Whisky is a lucky man."

"Thank you," Katya says graciously.

"Katya is a sailor from Russia. Your father has a boat charter business in Greece, doesn't he?"

"He does, He has many boats that he offers to tourists who want to explore the Greek islands," he says with pride.

"That sounds lovely, I've always wanted to sail the Greek Isles," Katya says.

Paul winks at me and says, "Whiskey, if you ever want to take Katya on a romantic trip to Greece, just let me know. I'll hook you up with one of my father's boats."

He smiles at me and says, "But for now, enjoy your dinner. And your date."

He leaves us alone and we look at each other. We both laugh and shake our heads.

"Paul is quite a character, isn't he?"

"He is. He's also very nice. And generous," she says appreciatively.

"He is. He's a good friend of mine. Do you want to go sailing?" I say teasingly.

"I do. And you know what? I'd love to go to Greece with you someday," she says boldly.

"Really? Well, then, maybe we should make that happen."

"Maybe we should," she says softly.

The rhythmic pulse of music fills the air as Katya and I approach Barracuda, my favorite night club in Puerto Morelos. I can't help but glance over at Katya, her dark hair dancing around her shoulders. She catches me looking and smiles, a mischievous glint in her eyes.

"Ready to meet my friends?" I ask, excitement bubbling up inside me as we step inside.

"Of course," she replies with confidence.

As we make our way to the bar, Hugo's guitar riffs cut through the air like a knife, captivating the crowd with his raw talent. He's on fire tonight, and I'll introduce him to Katya later. Although maybe not, all the women swoon over Hugo. Who needs that competition.

I'm reminded when I follow Katya's gaze locked on a dancer in front of Hugo. She is staring at the drop dead gorgeous, Natalie, dancing in front of Hugo, barely covering her curves with her skimpy outfit. She sure can dance though. She's a newcomer to Puerto Morelos and we often chat. She made a pass at me, but I knew better than to get involved. I owe it to her husband, who I'm told is a soldier serving his last tour overseas.

"Whiskey!" Nikos booms from behind the bar, his muscular arms expertly mixing drinks with practiced precision. He shoots me a knowing grin, clearly aware of the stunning woman by my side. "And who is this lovely lady?"

"Katya, meet Nikos," I say, gesturing to the towering Greek man. "He makes the best cocktails in town."

"Nice to meet you," Katya says, extending her hand. Nikos takes it gently, an unexpected softness in his grip, and bows his head slightly.

"Pleased to meet you," he replies, his deep voice full of friendliness. "What can I get you to drink?"

"Two margaritas, por favor," I answer.

As we wait for our drinks, I spot my friends gathered around a table near the dance floor. They're laughing and chatting animatedly. "Come on," I say to Katya, taking her hand. "Let's join the others."

"Whiskey, you old dog!" Bob exclaims as we approach, his eyes widening at the sight of Katya. "Who's your friend?"

"Everyone, this is Katya, my new Russian friend," I announce, beaming with pride. "Katya, meet Brian and Rosa, Bob and Becca, Josh and Karlie."

Brian, a former MI6 agent, eyes Katya warily because of her Russian origin. He says to Whisky, "So, this is your new friend, huh? Where did you meet her? And what does she do for a living?" He tries to sound casual, but his tone is laced with suspicion and hostility. He doesn't trust Katya, and he wonders if she has ulterior motives for being with Whiskey.

Rosa, Brian's Mexican wife senses the tension and invites Katya to sit next to her. Katya smiles warmly and takes the seat next to Rosa. The ice is broken quickly as Karlie enthusiastically shares the news of a Sunday bocce ball tournament and invites Katya to play. Katya's intelligence and beauty drew everyone in, and I could tell they were captivated by her presence.

As the night wears on, we take turns dancing, laughing, and sharing stories. The connection between Katya and me only grows stronger.

"Would you like some fresh air?" I ask her after a particularly energetic number. She nods, and I lead her to the street, the cool night air a welcome reprieve from the heat of the club.

"Tonight has been fun, Whiskey," she says, her eyes shimmering under the starry sky. "Thank you for introducing me to your friends. They are nice people."

Our eyes lock, and I feel a magnetic pull drawing us closer. As our lips meet. The kiss lingers. Slowly, I pull away, my eyes still closed, savouring the sensation. When I open them, I catch a fleeting expression of concern on Katya's face. It's gone as quickly as it appeared, replaced by her enchanting smile.

"Is everything okay?" I ask.

"Of course," she replies, her hand brushing against my cheek. "I just... I have to make a quick phone call."

"Sure, go ahead."

As she dials, I walk further out into the street. The the moon and stars shimmer overhead, casting a celestial glow, It's a breathtaking sight, one that has always brought me solace.

"да, это я" (Yes, it's me), I hear Katya speaking softly. "все идет по плану" (Everything is going according to plan). Her words are hushed, but I can't help overhearing her conversation. Even though I don't understand what she's saying, there is a sudden shift in her demeanour.

"Whiskey?" Her voice snaps me out of my thoughts.

"Nothing serious, I hope?" I ask, trying to keep my tone light, despite the questions swirling in my mind.

"No, just a small issue. It's all taken care of now," she assures me, her smile returning. "Now, where were we?"

"Right here," I say, pulling her close for another kiss. I can't help but wonder about the woman who is quickly capturing my heart. There's a mystery about her that both intrigues and worries me.

~

"Whiskey! Over here!" Bob calls out, waving me and Katya over to his and Becca's corner table at El Nicho.

"Morning, everyone," I greet them cheerfully, I hold the chair for Katya to take a seat, who flashes her captivating smile at me. Just weeks ago, she came into my life like a dream.

"Did you two lovebirds have another romantic evening?" Becca teases, raising an eyebrow. We share a laugh, and I feel a warmth in my chest.

"Something like that," I respond playfully, wrapping an arm around her waist. But as I look into her eyes, I can't shake the nagging feeling that something's not right. There's a flicker of something, a shadow that dances behind her gaze.

"Hey, Katya, tell us about your trip to Europe last year. Whiskey mentioned you traveled solo through France and Italy?" Becca asks. Her curiosity is innocent enough, but I can't help but notice how Katya's expression becomes guarded.

"Uh, yes. It was quite an adventure," she says hesitantly, avoiding eye contact. "I went to Rome and Paris, I love art and architecture."

But her words don't match the memories she'd shared with me just days ago. She had mentioned Venice and Paris not Rome and Paris. I try to brush off my concerns, but they fester in the back of my mind, gnawing at me.

"Katya, after breakfast, would you like to join me on a walk to the pier?" I ask, hoping for some privacy to voice my suspicions.

"Of course," she responds sweetly, taking my hand.

As we walk to the pier, not wanting to delay any longer.

"Katya, I have to ask... Is there something you're not telling me?" The words spill out before I can stop them, and she stiffens beside me.

"Whiskey, what do you mean?" Her innocent façade remains intact, but I can see the flicker of panic in her eyes.

"Your stories, Katya. They don't add up. You've told me different things at different times, and it's making me question who you really are," I admit, feeling the weight of my doubts crushing me.

"Whiskey, please..." She trails off, seemingly lost for words. "It's just... It's difficult to translate my thoughts to English."

"Is it, though?" I wonder unable to let it go. "Or is there something more going on?" I make a mental note to get a background check on Katya as soon as I get back to the villa.

The salty sea breeze tugs at my hair as I lead Katya along the shore, hoping that maybe we can find some clarity within the familiar setting. But as we approach Dive Bar, I notice a group of people huddled around the bar, their faces obscured by Josh's open laptop. He often does some market stuff in the morning but not with an audience.

"Whiskey! You've got to see this!" beckons Josh, his finger pointing urgently at the screen. "BREAKING NEWS!"

As I peer over his shoulder, I see Anderson Cooper on CNN. He is talking about the risk of Global Warfare. The bottom of the screen scrolls by and reads - Tensions escalate in the Ukrainian-Russian war. Drones were used to attack two oil pipeline installations in western Russia. The targets were the Druzhba pipeline, which carries oil from Russia to Europe, and the Togliatti-Odesa pipeline, which transports ammonia from Russia to Ukraine. The attacks caused explosions, fires, and damage to the pipelines and their facilities. Russia accused Ukraine of sabotage and terrorism, and threatened to retaliate. Ukraine denied any involvement in the attacks, and claimed they were staged by Russia to justify its aggression.

"Whiskey? Is everything okay?" Katya's voice startles me out of my thoughts, and I realize that she's now standing beside me, her gaze locked onto the screen.

Katya watched as Whiskey rushed off in a hurry, his voice rising with each word he spoke into the phone. "Whiskey," she called out, but he didn't seem to hear her. He gave her a final sharp glance and then he was gone, leaving Katya alone, thinking, "какого черта?' "What the fuck!"

Chapter 2
THE BETRAYAL

The sun beats down on my wrinkled forehead as I lounge by the pool, sipping a bourbon rocks. The salty sea breeze does little to cool the sweltering midday heat, but it's not the temperature that has me sweating.

"Damn Russians," I mutter under my breath, thinking about the recent pipeline bombings in Russia. With every explosion, the global oil economy teeters closer to chaos. As an old oil man, I know firsthand how unstable things can get when supply chains are disrupted. But this isn't just about money; it's about the balance of power in the world.

"Whiskey, amigo, you're looking mighty serious there," calls Josh coming up from the beach. He takes a swig from his bottle, wiping the condensation off with his Hawaiian shirt and joins me.

"Ah, just thinking about the news, Josh" I reply, forcing a smile. It's been a while since I've had to worry about this sort of thing. My life in Puerto Morelos has become a peaceful haven, far away from the cutthroat world of oil, politics and corporate espionage. Here, it's all about fishing trips, bocce ball, barbecues, and late-night card games.

"Those bombings, huh?" Josh shakes his head. "I don't envy those folks in the Ukrain right now. But hey, we got our own piece of paradise here!" He raises his beer bottle in a toast, and I clink mine against it, trying to focus on the good times we've shared in this sleepy coastal town.

"Yeah, you're right," I say. "We're lucky to be here." And it's true. Since stepping aside from the high-stakes world of oil pipeline engineering, my life has been filled with laughter, friendship, and the simple pleasures only a small Mexican town can offer. It's everything I ever wanted after years of high-powered boardrooms and clandestine operations.

"Speaking of luck," Josh grins, "I hear there's going to be a group for poker at Habs (Cantina) tonight. You in?"

"Wouldn't miss it," I reply, pushing thoughts of pipeline bombings to the back of my mind. After all, worrying about something on the other side of the globe won't change anything. Right now, the only thing that matters is living the good life here in Puerto Morelos, surrounded by the people I've come to call my family.

~

The sun sinks low on the horizon, casting long shadows across the sand as I make my way down to Cantina Habaneros.

"Hey, Whiskey!" Josh calls out, grinning ear to ear as he spots me entering the cantina. "You made it!"

I grinned at them and said, "Who's ready to lose some money?". They're already deep into a round of Texas hold'em, with laughter and good-natured ribbing filling the air.

My mind drifts back to Katya Rublev, the mysterious Russian woman I'd been seeing for less than a month. She was smart, beautiful, and always seemed to know exactly what to say. But there was something off about her, something that had always nagged at the edges of my mind. Her sudden disappearance only fueled my suspicions.

"Whiskey? You in or out?" Josh snaps his fingers in front of my face, pulling me back to the present.

"Sorry, guys. Just got a lot on my mind," I mumble, tossing some chips into the pot.

"Is this about Katya?" Karlie asks, concern etched on her face. "You know she wasn't right for you."

"Maybe not," I say, my voice barely more than a whisper. "But maybe she was after something else altogether."

"Like what?" Josh raises an eyebrow.

"Documents. Important ones," I confess, feeling a knot tighten in my chest. "After Katya disappeared, I had diagnostics done on my computer. It was just confirmed this evening, my computer was breached and files were downloaded."

"Fuck," Josh mutters, his eyes widening. "You think she took them?"

"More like stole them," I reply. "And now that I think about it, her timing was too perfect. The bombings in Russia, the world's attention on the oil industry... She must have been sent to target me specifically."

"Are you sure, Whiskey?" Brian asks, his voice laced with worry. "That's a pretty serious accusation."

"Unfortunately, I'm sure. The techies back in Houston know what to look for. The fact is, she played me like a fiddle."

"Shit," Josh curses, slamming his fists on the table. "You gotta watch your back, man."

"Believe me, I know, but right now, I need to figure out who Katya, really is, and what she was after and why. If she's tied to those bombings, then there's a lot more at stake than just my safety."

"Whatever you need, we've got your back," Karlie says, placing a hand on my shoulder.

"Thanks," I reply, grateful for their unwavering support.

The thought of Russia's involvement in their own pipeline bombings weighs heavily on my mind, and I'm certain there's more to it than meets the eye.

"Whiskey, you really think the Russians are behind this?" Karlie asks, her brow furrowed in worry.

"Look," I say, turning to face her, "you don't spend as much time in the oil industry as I have without learning a thing or two about how these bastards work."

"Like what?" Josh interjects, his arms crossed over his chest.

"Oil's their lifeblood," I explain, my voice low and serious. "It's not just about the money — it's about power and control. Russia has been playing this game for decades, and they're damn good at it."

"Alright, so let's say they are behind the bombings," Josh concedes. "What do they stand to gain?"

"Chaos, disrupt the global oil supply, manipulate prices, destabilize economies... For them, it's all part of the grand plan."

"Geezus," Josh mutters, running a hand through his hair. "And now you're caught up in the middle of it because of that woman."

"Seems that way but I'll be damned if I let them use me to further their agenda."

My concern for the global oil economy is palpable. The world may see me as an old man living out his retirement in Mexico, but I'll always feel the weight of my past and the responsibility I carry.

"Alright, so what's the plan?" Josh asks, his expression resolute.

"First things first," I say, my mind racing with possibilities. "We need to gather any and all information we can on Katya, her connections, and these bombings. Hell, if we're lucky, we might just find something that proves Russia's involvement."

"Sounds like a hell of a mission," Josh says, his eyes gleaming with determination.

"Damn straight it is," I reply, feeling a renewed sense of purpose surge through me. "But if there's one thing I've learned over the years, it's that you never back down from a challenge – especially when the stakes are this high."

I stroll out to the pier for some fresh air. The moon casting its glow upon the ocean as I cross my arms and lean against a palm tree. Waves lap at the shore, a soothing backdrop to the chaos unfolding in my mind.

"Whiskey," Josh calls out as he comes to join me, "you've gotta stop beating yourself up, man."

I shake my head, feeling the weight of my mistakes. "How could I have been so careless? Since stepping back from the company, I let my guard down – I practically rolled out the red carpet for Katya."

"Nobody could've seen this coming," he says. But it's not enough to ease the knot of guilt tightening in my gut.

"Maybe not," I admit, "but I should've known better. Why would a woman like Katya be with an old guy like me? Now, because of me, the war in the Ukrain will get worse and more innocent lives will be lost."

"Whiskey, you're one of the smartest, most resourceful people I know," Josh reassures me, placing a hand on my shoulder. "If anyone can find the truth out of this mess, it's you."

"Thanks, Josh," I say, nodding resolutely. "I need to find out everything we can about Katya, her connections, and the bombings. I won't rest until I prove she's a spy and expose Russia's involvement."

"I can help," he responds, a determined glint in his eyes.

My friends and I may be living in paradise, but there's a storm brewing on the horizon, and I intend to face it head-on. For the sake of the Ukraine, the global oil economy and for the world at large, I'll bring the truth to light.

~

I take a deep breath, the salty air filling my lungs, before pulling out my phone. It's time to call in some favors. As I scroll through my contacts, I find Steve Stevens, the head of the FBI and U.S. counterpart for The Five Eyes alliance. The Five Eyes alliance is an intelligence-sharing network made up of the US, UK, Canada, Australia and New Zealand. It was established after World War II as a way to monitor China and Russia, and share classified information. It is often considered the most successful intelligence alliance in the world. Steve and I go way back, working together on numerous issues throughout the years. He's someone I've always trusted but these days, it seems like trust is a scarce commodity.

"Steve, it's Whiskey," I say as soon as he picks up. "I need your help."

"Whiskey? Well, it's been a while," Steve responds, his voice heavy with surprise. "How's retirement treating you?"

"No time for small talk," I cut in, urgency leaking into my tone. "I've stumbled onto something big, and I think it's connected to those pipeline bombings in Russia."

"Slow down, buddy," Steve says, his casual tone grating against my nerves. "What exactly do you think you found?"

I quickly recount my relationship with Katya Rublev, the breach of my computer and the stolen documents, and my growing suspicion that she's a Russian spy. There's a tense silence on the other end of the line as Steve processes the information.

"Whiskey, I don't know what to tell you, man," he finally says, sounding unconvinced. "It sounds like you might be jumping to conclusions here."

The Betrayal

"Jumping to conclusions?" I snap, frustration boiling inside me. "I'm telling you, Steve, there's something going on, and if we don't act fast, there could be major repercussions for the global oil economy and the war in Ukraine. The documents she stole contain agreements with Governments regarding the ownership, operation, and security of their pipelines and the oil fields that supply them. Financial records that show volume, value, and destination of the oil exported through pipelines. Maps, diagrams, and technical specifications of pipelines and the oil wells that feed them. All the information anyone would want to know if they are planning an attack on a pipeline. I didn't have documents on the Russian pipelines that were recently bombed. So I don't know how that fits but I have lots of information on other pipelines all around the globe."

"Look, I get it," Steve replies, the placating tone in his voice making my blood boil. "You're worry might be justified. But we can't just go off half-cocked based on a hunch. You've been out of the game for a while, Whiskey. Maybe you're just seeing shadows where there aren't any."

I clench, anger and disappointment warring within me. I never thought Steve would brush off my concerns like this. "This isn't just about finding the truth about Katya," I growl, the words bitter in my mouth. "It's about doing what's right."

"Whiskey, I hear you," he says with a sigh. "But we can't act without solid evidence. If you find something more concrete, then give me a call."

"Fine," I spit out before hanging up. My trust in the U.S. government, already shaky, has taken another hit. It seems like I'm truly on my own in this mess. But that doesn't mean I'm going to give up. Course not. It just means I'll have to rely on my own resourcefulness, friends and contacts. With or without Steve's help, I'm determined to uncover the truth and expose Katya. And if Russia is behind the bombings, or planning future bombings they're going to answer for it – I'll make damn sure of that.

~

A plan starts to form in my mind as I pace around my villa. I'm done waiting for someone else to make a move. It's time to take matters into my own hands.

"Alright, Whiskey, think," I mutter under my breath, forcing myself to focus on the task at hand. "You've got resources here in Puerto Morelos. You just need to rally them."

I grab my phone and start tapping out messages to the expats – people I know I can trust, who've got skills and resources to bring to the table. The more eyes we have on this situation, the better.

"Whiskey, what's going on?" comes Brian Stone's voice through the phone speaker, concern lacing his words. I'd reached out to him first, knowing that if anyone could help me devise a strategy, it'd be him. He's an ex MI6 agent. He married a Mexican woman Rosa, they met and live in Ibiza. Seems Rosa might have fled to Ibiza to avoid her familial connections to the Sinaloa Cartel. Now they spend a couple months a year in Puerto Morelos, where Rosa gets a chance to catch up with her daughters and mother.

"Brian, I need your help," I say, my voice low but firm. "Something big is happening, and I think Russia might be involved. We need to gather evidence and expose them."

"This about the pipeline bombings?" he asks concern in his voice.

"Katya Rublev," I explain, my gut twisting at the mention of her name. "She was using me, Brian. She stole documents from my computer and then there were bombings in Russia. I can't shake the feeling that she's connected."

"Right," Brian says after a pause, his voice colder than a Moscow winter. "We'll find her, Whiskey. And we'll gather enough evidence to prove whatever she's up to."

"Thank you, I knew I could count on you."

"Always, mate," he replies. "So, what's our plan?"

"First, we need to locate Katya," I say, my thoughts racing as the pieces begin to fall into place. "Bob and Becca with their cyber security and hacking abilities can help us. We'll start by digging through CCTV at the Cancun airport and we won't stop until we find her. Josh and Karlie will be helpful as well. We gather evidence," I say, my determination growing stronger by the second. "We watch her every move, tap her phone, monitor her communications — whatever it takes to prove that she's a spy and expose Russia's role in all this."

"Sounds like a plan," he says, his voice carrying that familiar edge of excitement that I know means he's already mentally preparing for the mission ahead. "I'll be there as soon as I can, Whiskey. We'll get to the bottom of this together."

"Good, I'll be waiting."

As I hang up, my heart pounds in my chest, adrenaline coursing through my veins. This isn't just about me anymore — it's about protecting the world from whatever nefarious plot is unfolding. Together, with my trusted friends at my side, we're going to expose the truth.

I walk out onto the balcony of my villa, taking in the view of the ocean. It's hard to believe that this peaceful life I've built for myself was compromised by the dark underbelly of espionage. My bare feet pad across the sun-warmed tiles as I begin to pace, thinking of the dangers that lie ahead.

"Whiskey," Brian says, appearing beside me, his eyes filled with concern. "We're going to need to tighten security around here. We can't afford any slip-ups."

"You're right," I reply, my voice firm. "We need to protect ourselves."

"Exactly," he nods. "So, we'll install surveillance cameras, set up alarms, and make sure everyone has a secure communication channel. We need to be prepared for anything."

"Agreed." I feel the weight of responsibility settle on my shoulders. These are my people – my friends – and I'll do whatever it takes to keep them safe.

As we stand there, side by side, I watch the undulating waves. This place, once a sanctuary from the chaos of the world, has been infiltrated by shadows. Gone are the days of carefree laughter and shared stories over tequila sunsets. Instead, we're now thrust into a world filled with lies, deceit, and danger.

As we walk back inside, my heart swells with determination. Russia may have struck the first blow, but they won't win this battle.

~

The Betrayal

"Whiskey," Brian calls from behind me, his tone urgent. "You've got a call from Steve Stevens."

"About damn time," I mutter under my breath, heading inside. My thoughts race as I pick up the phone, wondering if Steve has had a change of heart or if he's still brushing off my concerns. Either way, I'm ready to confront him.

"Steve, what have you got for me?" I demand without preamble.

"Whiskey, I owe you an apology," he says, his voice tense. "I've looked into it further, and you might be right. Something might be going on."

Frustration still simmering beneath the surface. But the fact that he's come around brings a renewed determination to see this through.

"Can you send me all the intel you've gathered so far," Steve instructs.

"Understood," I say, hanging up the phone before turning to face Brian. "We're not alone in this anymore. Steve's finally on board."

"Good to hear," Brian nods, relief flickering across his face. "Now we've got a fighting chance. I'll go to Cancun now and get security equipment. I'll meet you at La Sirena rooftop this evening."

Chapter 3
THE PLAN BEGINS

The sun fades, bathing the beach in soft pink. It's as if the air itself is pink. On the rooftop at La Sirena, nursing a glass of whiskey in one hand as I do every evening. My old bones creak as I settle into my stool at the end of the bar, waiting for Brian Stone to arrive.

"Whiskey," a voice calls out. Brian emerges, his tall frame casting an ominous silhouette against the dwindling sunlight. His piercing blue eyes flicker with intensity, and I can tell he's already in mission mode.

"Evening, Brian." I take a swig of my drink, savoring the burn before setting the glass down on the table.

"First things first," Brian says, his voice low and cautious. He pulls a small device from his pocket and begins scanning the area for listening bugs. I watch him work, admiring the efficiency and precision that comes from years of experience as an MI6 agent. Trusting him has never been an issue.

The Plan Begins

"Clear," he announces after a few moments, pocketing the device. He takes a seat across from me, his gaze sharp and focused. "Alright, Whiskey. Let's talk strategy."

I nod, leaning forward in my chair. "We need to find Katya, figure out what she and her handlers are up to, and gather evidence against them all. I've got some ideas, but I'm open to suggestions."

Brian rubs his chin thoughtfully, his eyes narrowing as he considers our options. "Your instincts have served you well so far, Whiskey. I say we follow your lead."

"I don't know about that," I allow myself a small smile.

"Brian," I say, my voice low and gravelly, "I trust your expertise more than anyone else's. But this Katya situation... it's the big leagues. She's infiltrated our lives, and these Russian pipeline bombings have me on edge."

His eyes lock onto mine, a silent acknowledgment of the gravity of the situation. "Whiskey, I understand." He shifts on his stool, the wood creaking beneath him. "We'll gather the evidence we need against her. And get it to Steve Stevens."

I nod, feeling a flicker of relief at his reassurance. "Ok, let's figure out where she might be hiding and how to get close enough without raising suspicion."

"Patience and observation are key here," Brian advises.

The clink of ice cubes in my glass punctuates the silence as I take a sip of my drink. Brian's eyes remain focused on the map he is viewing on his iPad, his brow furrowed in concentration. "We have to consider her connections and resources," he says, tapping a finger against his chin.

"Considering her knowledge of you and your movements, it's possible she knows we'll be onto her. We'll need to work fast." He stands gazing out at the leaning lighthouse, the ocean, the moon above. "What about Bob and Becca? Have you recruited them?"

"Yes, Becca's excited and in her element but Bob is more concerned. We need to be cautious in involving them. Their safety could be compromised if Katya catches onto their involvement."

"Agreed. But they're smart, they know how to cover their tracks. If anyone can hack security systems it's them. Remember, Whiskey, we're relying on Bob and Becca, we need to trust they know what they are doing."

I glance at Brian, his gaze locked on the iPad, as though he's already plotting our next move. His sharp mind is always three steps ahead, and I know he's searching for any advantage we can get.

"Whiskey," Brian says, shifting his attention to me. "I have an idea. My connections in the intelligence community can still get us access to classified databases and surveillance footage, if Bob and Becca hit a wall or need assistance, I can reach out to them."

I nod, impressed by his resourcefulness. "That's brilliant, Brian. We could use all the help we can get."

"However," he adds, his piercing blue eyes reflecting concern, "there are risks involved. If we're caught snooping around classified information, it won't just be Russian spies we need to worry about."

"Who else?" I ask, my gut twisting with unease.

The Plan Begins

"Old friends who don't take kindly to former agents poking their noses where they don't belong," Brian replies, his voice heavy with implication. "I've made my fair share of enemies over the years, Whiskey. This mission could put us in their crosshairs."

"It's a risk we have to take, Brian. There's too much at stake here. We need to find Katya. My computer suffered such a massive breach that I suspect the recent bombings are not the ultimate aim.

"Agreed," he says, his expression resolute. "But we must tread carefully, alerting neither our old adversaries nor the Russians," a slight smile tugging at the corner of his mouth. "Just remember, Whiskey, trust no one but ourselves. Everyone else is a potential threat."

"Understood."

"Alright then," Brian says, extending his hand for a firm shake. "Let's get to work."

As we exchange a determined grip, I can't help but feel that, despite the risks, we still have a fighting chance. Together, we'll find Katya and expose Russia's plot.

"Whiskey," he says, "We need to approach Katya in a way that won't spook her. If we can gain her trust, we might be able to gather more evidence. My sense is she is not a cold blooded killer."

"But how do we get close to her without tipping her off? She's a trained spy, after all."

"True," Brian replies, "I have an idea."

"God help us," I mutter under my breath.

Chapter 4
ALL HANDS ON DECK

Whiskey stands at the floor-to-ceiling windows of his Puerto Morelos villa, eyes fixed on the horizon. The swish of the palm trees, murmurs from the conversation behind him, it's time to get to it. He turns, facing the roomful of expats – his team.

"Alright, everybody," I say, clapping my hands together. "We've got a mission ahead of us. We need to figure out who's bombing oil pipelines. Let's divvy up the tasks and get this show on the road."

Bob Thompson, sitting in his favorite armchair, nods slowly, a determined glint in his aging eyes. His fingers twitch with anticipation, eager to dig into the tech side of things.

"Whiskey, I'll get started on securing our communications," Bob says as he pulls out his laptop. "We have to make sure no one's listening in on us."

"Good thinking, Bob." I watch as he expertly navigates the laptop, setting up firewalls on our computers, iPads, and phones. It's a sight that leaves me awestruck – this old man, fighting the decline of his mind, still retaining enough knowledge to keep us safe in this digital age.

As Bob works, I take a moment to survey the others present, each of them bringing their own unique skill set to the table.

The room vibrates with quiet tension as Bob continues his work, the click-clack of his keyboard punctuating each focused breath. I lean in closer, my heart pounding like a restless drum, and watch his fingers dance across the keys.

"Okay, folks," Bob announces, wiping beads of sweat from his brow. "I've got our devices locked down tight. Now pay attention, because this is crucial: we need strong, unique passwords for everything. No 'password123' garbage. And don't use your dog's name or your favorite football team either."

"Got it, Bob," murmurs Josh, nodding seriously behind his spectacles. He's posted up at the dining table with his laptop, already tracking any suspicious monetary transactions related to the bombings. Looking to see who, if anyone, made a sudden fortune from the stock market's reaction to the bombings. 'Always follow the money', is Josh's motto.

"Encryption is just as important, if not more so," Bob stresses, his voice cracking with urgency. "We're dealing with dangerous people, capable of unimaginable things. If they intercept our communications without encryption, we're toast."

"Please Bob, for the rest of us, what the heck is encryption?" asks Rosa.

"Encryption is a way of hiding information by changing it into a secret code that only authorized parties can understand," Bob explains patiently.

"Understood?" I ask the group, my gut churning at the thought of what could happen if we slip up. Trusting these friends of mine is one thing, but trusting technology? That's another story.

Josh's fingers fly over his keyboard, his analytical mind processing data faster than I could ever hope to. His balding head beaded with sweat as he leans in, scrutinizing every detail on his screen. The weight of the world seems to rest on his broad shoulders, but I know that if anyone can find the answers we need, it's him.

"Whiskey, I'm seeing some unusual transactions here," Josh calls out, his brow furrowing. "Might be nothing, but it's worth looking into."

"Keep digging, Josh," I encourage, "every scrap of information helps. Guys, remember," I say, my voice low and steady. "This isn't just about bombings - it's about exposing the Russians.

I watch Josh, eyes glued to the screen. My curiosity gets the best of me; I need to understand what he's doing. "Josh," I say, leaning in, "walk me through your process. How are you analyzing the financial data?"

"Sure, Whiskey," Josh replies, adjusting his spectacles. "First, I gather as much information as possible from various sources - banks, investment firms, even the dark web. Then, I create a database and run algorithms to identify patterns, anomalies, or anything that might raise a red flag."

"Like those unusual transactions you mentioned earlier?"

"Exactly." He nods, pointing at his screen. "These transactions could be linked to who cashed out somehow. It's like finding a needle in a haystack, but once we've got something solid, it'll be worth it."

"Keep up the good work, buddy," I pat him on the back, feeling reassured by his expertise.

Turning my attention to the rest of the room, I realize everyone is waiting for guidance. It's time to get this investigation moving.

"Alright, team," I say with authority, "listen up. I'm going to assign each of you a specific task based on your expertise. We need everyone actively involved so we can cover as much ground as possible."

Heads nod in agreement, their faces etched with determination.

"Bob, continue securing our communications. Becca, track Katya's movements on the CCTV at the Cancun airport, let's see where she flew off to. Rosa, reach out to your friends and contacts and see if they know anything about Russian operatives in Mexico, particularly Puerto Morelos/Cancun area. And Karlie, use your journalistic skills to monitor foreign, domestic and social media outlets for any leads.

"Got it, Whiskey," they chime in unison.

With that, we get to work - a well-oiled machine of diverse talents and skills, all focused on a single goal. I can't help but feel a sense of pride as I watch my friends in action, each one playing their part in this high-stakes investigation.

"Bob announces, his voice filled with pride, "I've finished the firewalls and our communications should be secure now. Time for a test run."

Bob opens an encrypted messaging app on his laptop and sends a message to each of us. A satisfying chime rings out from everyone's devices as we receive the test message.

"Good job, Bob," I praise him, knowing how vital this protection is for our mission.

"Thanks, Whiskey," he replies with a grin, the twinkle in his eyes reminiscent of his younger years.

"Guys, I've found something you all need to see," Josh interjects, his voice heavy with concern. We gather around his laptop, our collective curiosity piqued.

"Look at these transactions," Josh says, showing a series of numbers on his screen. "Several American accounts purchased a substantial amount of stock in major U.S. oil and gas companies just before the pipeline bombings. After the bombings they made a ton of money as these stocks were a beneficiary of the crisis in Europe's oil market. This suggests that they knew about the bombings and profited from them. This contradicts the Russian narrative of bombing their own pipelines."

"Josh," Karlie mutters, her eyes wide with disbelief. "You're saying some Americans made money off these attacks?"

"Seems so," Josh confirms, adjusting his spectacles with a sigh. "Looks like too significant an amount to be a coincidence."

"Could be an inside job," Becca suggests, her sharp instincts kicking in. "Someone with ties to both countries making a profit off of chaos."

"Exactly my thoughts," I agree, running a hand through my hair. "We can't jump to any conclusions yet. Josh, keep checking for any other big payoffs on the other side of the pond?"

I take a deep breath, feeling the weight of our discovery. "Let's take a short break, everyone. Grab some snacks and refreshments. We'll reconvene in thirty."

My friends disperse, stretching their legs and rummaging through the kitchen for sustenance. I pour myself a stiff drink, the ice clinking against the glass as I swirl it around. My mind races with thoughts...what is going on here?

"Hey, Josh," Karlie calls out from across the room, her voice full of concern. She holds a plate of fruit and cheese, her bright red hair falling over her shoulder as she leans against the counter. "Can I ask you something?"

"Sure thing, Karlie," Josh replies, removing his glasses and rubbing the bridge of his nose. He's tired, but there's no denying the fire burning in his eyes – a fire fueled by determination and a thirst for truth.

"How do you deal with all this?" Karlie asks, gesturing vaguely to the laptop. "All this... darkness? Don't you ever just want to paint the world in brighter colors?"

Josh smiles faintly, nodding his head. "Sometimes, maybe. But this is the reality of the world. It's what gives us leverage. With leverage we can make a difference, to improve the world, if that's what we choose."

Karlie smiles, nodding in understanding. "I guess that makes sense. It's just hard, knowing money and greed, is always lurking beneath the surface."

"Indeed," Josh agrees, his expression sobering. "But that's the world we live in, like it or not."

The room falls silent for a moment. We thought we left all this behind when we came to live in paradise.

"Alright," I announce, setting my empty glass on the counter. "Let's get back to it."

My friends gather around once more, their expressions resolute and focused. "Remember," I tell them, my voice steady but firm, "our safety is paramount. We're up against powerful forces, and they'll stop at nothing to protect their interests. Be careful and trust no one but each other."

"Understood, Whiskey," Bob replies, his fingers already flying over his keyboard as he resumes his work. The others nod in agreement, determination etched across their faces. As we delve deeper into our investigation, I can't shake the nagging feeling that we're treading on dangerous ground.

The sound of Rosa clearing her throat pulls me back into the present, my thoughts momentarily silenced. She looks around nervously, as if debating whether to speak up or not. Then, she takes a deep breath and plunges forward.

"Whiskey," she begins, her voice wavering slightly, "there's something I should tell you. My contact who is connected to the cartel said they heard whispers a long while back of a Russian enforcer in Puerto Morelos."

All Hands on Deck

"Cartel?" Karlie exclaims, her eyes wide with shock. "Rosa, do you really think it's wise to involve them in this?"

"Desperate times call for desperate measures," Rosa replies, her expression resolute.

Weighing the risks against the potential benefits. "The last thing we need is to get tangled up with the cartel on top of everything else."

Rosa nods, relief flooding her features. "I just wanted you all to know that this what they heard."

"Thanks, Rosa," I reply, appreciating her willingness to help.

Bob speaks up first, his brow furrowed as he considers his words carefully. "Whiskey, what's our exit strategy? We need to make sure we have a solid plan for getting out of Mexico if they come for us."

"Good point, Bob," I agree, feeling a surge of gratitude for his foresight. "Our best bet is to stay under the radar as much as possible, using our individual skills to navigate any obstacles that come our way. I'll contact my private security team in Houston, get them to send a team here right away to oversee our protection. And if all else fails, we'll rely on Brian and his wits to help get us out of a bind."

"Alright, I can work with that," Bob nods, seemingly satisfied with my answer.

"Anyone else?" I ask, scanning the room for any lingering doubts or fears.

When no one else speaks up, I take that as a sign that we're as prepared as we can be.

Brian heads to the terrace, his blue eyes focused and intense as he mentally rehearses his role in the mission. I know he'll be responsible for securing our exit if things go south, and I have no doubt he's up to the task.

"Keep your comms open," he reminds me. "We need to stay connected at all times."

"Understood," I nod.

Bob and Becca huddle together in the atrium, working in tandem to trace Katya's movements. Bob's face is etched with lines of worry.

"Stay strong, Bob," I encourage him. "We need your expertise."

"Thanks, Whiskey," he replies, a spark of determination in his eyes. "I won't let you down."

"Nor will I," Becca chimes in, her steady presence a comfort to us all.

I take one last glance around the room, locking eyes with each member of my team. I pray we are not caught snooping around. The Russians would not think twice about eliminating the lot of us.

Chapter 5
SECURITY TEAM ARRIVES

Whiskey mutters under his breath, "time to call Houston."

He fishes out his old clamshell phone from his pocket – a relic from the past that's never let him down.

I glance at the security company's number on the screen of my phone, time to get down to business. I clear my throat and hit the call button. "Whiskey Black here, I need your assistance."

"Mr. Black," comes the reply, "of course, we're here to support you. What do you need?"

"Protection for my villa in Puerto Morelos and my people," I say, my eyes darting around the villa as I take in the faces of my friends. Their lives are in my hands now, and I won't let them down. "We're going up against some formidable adversaries."

"Understood, Mr. Black," the voice responds, all business. "We'll provide the necessary support. Can you give us more details about the situation and potential risks?"

"Alright." I sigh, steeling myself for what I need to divulge. "We've got ourselves tangled up in some international espionage. The kind of stuff that makes headlines when it goes wrong. We're dealing with powerful people who won't hesitate to eliminate anyone in their way."

"Thank you for sharing this information, Mr. Black," the voice says, reassurance threaded through their words. "We'll ensure that our team is prepared for these threats. Your safety is our priority."

"Good." I nod, my chest tightening. "I trust you'll keep this confidential."

"Absolutely, Mr. Black," the voice promises. "Our team will handle everything discreetly and professionally. You can count on us."

"Thanks. I'll be waiting for your team."

"I'll get back to you shortly with their ETA," they reply before ending the call.

I pocket my phone and look at my friends. The villa is silent, the air heavy with anticipation. I see the fear and uncertainty in their eyes, but also the determination. The sun hangs low in the sky, casting long shadows across the villa's courtyard. I can almost feel the tension crackling in the air as my friends gather around me, anticipation and fear mingling with the stifling heat.

Squinting at my phone's screen as I receive a text from the security company, "our security is en route. They'll be here soon."

Security Team Arrives

"Who are these guys, Whiskey?" asks Rosa, her fingers toying nervously with the frayed edges of her shorts. "Are they really going to be able to protect us?"

"Best in the business," I reply, keeping my eyes on the screen as I type out a response. "Highly trained professionals, all of them. We're in good hands." I don't mention the knot that's been twisting in my gut ever since I made the call. No need to worry them more than they already are.

"Okay," says Brian, his voice steady despite the dark circles under his eyes. "What do we need to do to prepare for their arrival?"

"Let's make sure the villa is ready for an influx of people," I suggest, setting my phone aside for a moment. "We'll need to clear some space for equipment, maybe move some furniture around. And let's stock up on food, water and other necessities—we don't know how long this is going to take."

"Got it," says Rosa, her tone determined as she wipes her brow with the back of her hand. 'I'll get started right away."

"Good," I nod, then turn my attention back to my phone as it buzzes with another message. I tap out a quick reply, coordinating details of the security team's arrival.

"Whiskey, you sure about this?" asks Bob. "These guys... they're gonna be armed, right?"

"Of course, but they're here to protect us, remember? We need their expertise, and we need it now."

"Right," Bob mutters, his gaze drifting off into the distance. "I just hope we're not biting off more than we can chew."

"Trust me, Bob," I say, clapping him on the shoulder. "We've got this."

~

The sun burns hot overhead, shimmering off the water as I wait for the security team to arrive. The air tastes like salt and anticipation, a sharp tang in my throat that won't go away. This is not the kind of life I'd planned on when I first came to Puerto Morelos.

"Whiskey," Bob says, his voice tense as he turns to me. "They're here."

I squint into the distance, and sure enough, two black SUVs, kicking up a cloud of dust behind them. They screech to a halt in front of the villa, and before I can take another breath, the doors fly open. Out step four men and one woman, all dressed in identical black pants and shirts and dark sunglasses. They look like they've stepped straight out of an action movie.

"Mr. Black?" the woman asks, extending her hand. "I'm Agent Santiago. We're here to help."

"Call me Whiskey," I tell her, shaking her firm grip. "Appreciate you coming down so quickly."

"Of course," she nods. "We understand the urgency of the situation."

"Let's get down to business," I say, gesturing to my expat friends gathered nearby. "This is my family, so to speak."

"Understood," Agent Santiago says, scanning the group with a practiced eye. "Our priority is your safety, but we'll do our best to minimize disruption."

"Good," I say, relieved.

We move inside my villa, where the team unpacks their gear and lays it out on the table. Radios, body armor, weapons—this is serious business. Agent Santiago talks us through the protocols, her voice steady but urgent.

"Communication is key," she says, looking each of us in the eye. "We'll be monitoring the situation closely and providing updates as necessary. But we need you to report anything suspicious immediately. Understood?"

My friends nod, their faces a mix of determination and uncertainty. I can't blame them; this is not what any of us signed up for when we fled our old lives for the tropical paradise of Puerto Morelos. But we're in the thick of it now, and there's no going back.

"Look," I say, stepping forward. "I know this is hard. We came here to escape, to live carefree. But until we know for certain there are no Russian hitman or spies around. I'm going to err on the side of caution" – I wave my hand toward the security team – "and the sooner we uncover why Katya came here to steal my documents, the sooner we get back to bocce ball on the beach."

"Here's to that," Karlie says.

As we dive into the nitty-gritty details of surveillance schedules and evacuation plans, I can't help but feel a fierce surge of pride in my makeshift investigative team. We may be a ragtag bunch of expats, but we've got grit.

As the security team gets to work. Agent Santiago takes the lead, her eyes scanning every inch of the property like a hawk. I follow close behind, feeling the weight of the responsibility settle heavy on my shoulders.

"Whiskey," she says, "our first priority is to assess any vulnerabilities or potential entry points. We need to make sure this place is locked down tight."

We walk the perimeter of the villa, the rest of the security team fanning out to check the surrounding area. Josh and Brian accompany them, their long strides betraying their eagerness to help.

"Here," Agent Santiago points to a palm tree leaning on the fence wall from the outside, "This could be an issue. We'll need to cut it down."

"Sure, no problem."

We continue our inspection, pointing out weak spots and discussing potential improvements. The security team works efficiently, their movements precise and methodical. It's clear they've done this before, and it's oddly comforting.

Over the next few hours, the security team installs surveillance cameras, alarm systems, and other high-tech gadgets throughout the property. They move with purpose, transforming the once carefree villa into a fortress.

"Whiskey, come take a look at this," Agent Santiago calls from the main entrance.

I approach and see that she's holding a tablet connected to the new surveillance system. On the screen, I can see every inch of the villa, monitored in real time.

"Damn," I mutter, impressed. "You guys don't mess around."

"Neither do the people we're up against," she replies, her smile fading. "We need to be prepared for anything."

"Right." I swallow hard, the reality of the situation hitting me like a freight train. This is not some game. Lives are on the line — my friends' lives.

With the sun now fully set, the security team finishes their work. Agent Santiago gathers everyone together for one final briefing.

"Remember," she says, her eyes locked on mine. "Communication is key. If you see anything suspicious, report it immediately. We're here to protect you."

I nod. "Alright, let's get some rest, tomorrow's another day."

~

The morning sun is a big bright yellow ball on the horizon. The scent of brewing coffee drifts out from the kitchen.

"Whiskey!" Karlie calls, beckoning me on the terrace. "Come, join us."

We sit around the heavy wooden table making small talk. Agent Santiago enters the room, her brisk stride betraying the urgency she feels. She sets down a small stack of laminated cards on the table, each emblazoned with emergency contact information.

"Listen up, everyone," she says, her piercing gaze sweeping the room. "These cards contain instructions on how to handle different scenarios you may encounter. We've covered everything from medical emergencies to potential threats. Familiarize yourselves with this information — keep it on your person - it could save your life."

"Thanks again for all your hard work, Agent Santiago. We appreciate everything you and your team have done for us."

"Of course," she nods, a ghost of a smile playing on her lips. "It's our job to keep you safe."

"Let's just hope we won't need to use any of this," Karlie murmurs, rubbing her thumb over the glossy surface of the card.

"Better to have it and not need it than to need it and not have it," Josh remarks sagely.

"True enough," I concede, "but let's not dwell on the what-ifs. We have work to do."

"Whiskey," Becca calls out from the atrium, her voice strained as she scans security footage, "I think we've got our next lead."

"Alright, bring it out, what have you found?"

"I've been tracking Katya's movements from Cancun airport where she boarded a flight for Frankfurt, from there, she went to Sochi. Doesn't look like she boarded another flight. This could be where she is now."

"Great work Becca! Well I'll be damned, maybe there was some truth in her cover story. Everyone, gather around."

As everyone converges at the table, I tell them about Katya's story of growing up in Sochi and sailing with her father.

"She mention she owned a sailboat called Katya's Dream. Obviously that's not going to be the name of her boat but from the way she spoke about sailing with her father in Sochi as a child, I might be wrong, but I don't think she made that up. Well, at least it's a place to start."

Security Team Arrives

"Brian, you will head to Sochi, immediately."

"I'm on it, I have contacts on the ground to assist in locating Katya, if she is still in Sochi. I'll find her."

Chapter 6
BRIAN ARRIVES IN SOCHI

As I step off the train onto Sochi's bustling platform, I can't help but feel an odd sense of exhilaration. The city is alive with activity, people rushing through the station like a river of humanity, each person carving their own unique path through the crowd. There's something about this place – a captivating energy that fuses the old world and the new. It feels simultaneously familiar and alien.

I weave my way through the throngs of people, taking in the smells of fresh-baked pastries from street vendors and the sound of laughter echoing off the walls. I notice the vibrant colors of the traditional Russian attire worn by some, while others sport designer jeans and flashy sunglasses. This fusion of East and West is intoxicating, and I can't help but feel drawn to it.

Despite the city's allure, I know I need to get down to business. Katya Rublev, the Russian spy I've been tasked with tracking down, could be somewhere in this city.

Brian Arrives in Sochi

As I make my way towards the sea terminal, I discreetly reach out to my network of local contacts. A few hurried phone calls later, and I'm armed with a list of likely locations where a Russian spy with a penchant for boating might live.

The sun begins to dip below the horizon, casting long shadows across the city streets as I zero in on a few key locations. I sit in-front of the window of a small cafe near one of the marinas, observing the comings and goings of boats and their owners. I find myself wondering what the real Katya is actually like in person - her mannerisms, her expressions, the way she might try to outwit me.

"Hey, Brian!" a voice calls out, snapping me back to reality. It's one of my contacts, a man named Yuri who runs a small fishing business. He approaches with a grin and a firm handshake. "I have something for you."

"I've managed to gather some information on your target: Katya Rublev, aka Zoya Petrov." He slides a small envelope across the table, careful not to draw attention. "She owns a boat, which makes it more difficult to pinpoint her exact location."

"Boat owners tend to gravitate towards certain locations, though," I muse, pocketing the envelope discreetly. "Places where they can dock, refuel, and resupply."

"True," Yuri nods, "but you'll need to be careful. Her connections run deep within the Russian government, and she has powerful friends."

"Then I'll just have to be more cunning than her friends," I say with a tight smile, thanking him for his assistance.

Over the next few days, I immerse myself in the world of Sochi's boat owners. I visit marinas, chat up dockworkers, and even pose as a potential buyer looking for a vessel. Each interaction brings me closer to my goal: finding Katya.

As the pieces begin to fall into place, I can't help but think about the woman at the center of it all. Who is she, really? A ruthless operative, or a pawn in a larger game? My instincts tell me there's more to her than meets the eye, and I'm determined to uncover the truth.

Finally, after days of tireless searching, I narrow down my list of potential locations to a single dock on the outskirts of the city. It's secluded, well-guarded, and home to a sleek black yacht that seems like the perfect hideout for a spy like Katya.

"Got you," I whisper to myself, feeling a surge of adrenaline as I see a familiar figure with a long black ponytail coming up from below deck. And so, with a deep breath, I plan to stake her out and approach her in a neutral location.

A slender figure threading her way through the crowd at the Sochi sea terminal. She moves with purpose and precision, her every step betraying a lifetime of training. There's no mistaking it; this is Katya.

Tracking her isn't easy; she's cautious, taking circuitous routes that would throw off most pursuers. But I'm not most pursuers, and I've come too far to lose her now. She leads me to the Brigantina Cafe, its inviting aroma wafting through the air as we approach. The cafe's cozy interior is a stark contrast to the brisk Russian winter outside, and its spacious terrace offers an unobstructed view of the sea. Locals and tourists alike fill the space, chatting animatedly over plates of steaming borscht and aromatic pizzas.

Brian Arrives in Sochi

Steeling myself for what comes next. "This is it." I watch as Katya takes a seat by the window, sipping on a cup of steaming black coffee. My heart races as I cross the threshold, feeling the weight of the situation bearing down on me. This woman is the key to unraveling the plot behind the Russian pipeline bombings, and I can't afford to make a misstep.

"Hello, Katya," I say, maintaining a calm and composed demeanor as I slide into the chair opposite her. Her eyes flicker up to meet mine, registering a brief moment of surprise before settling into a guarded expression.

"Why are you here Mr. Stone?" she asks, her voice low and tinged with suspicion.

"I think we have some common interests."

"Is that so?" she inquires, her gaze never leaving mine as she weighs her options.

"Indeed." I lean back in my chair, giving her room to breathe. "I know you're involved in something much bigger than yourself. I'm here to help you, if you'll let me."

"Help me?" she scoffs, her eyes narrowing. "And why should I trust you?"

"Because I don't think you really want innocent lives lost," I say, my voice steady and sincere, "That's not the woman I met in Puerto Morelos."

She considers this for a moment, her eyes searching mine for any hint of deception. The silence stretches on, the tension between us palpable.

"Alright," she finally murmurs, her guarded expression softening ever so slightly. "Let's talk."

As I delve into conversation with Katya, I'm acutely aware of the delicate balance we're walking. A single misstep could send her back into the shadows. But for now, at least, it seems I've gained her trust. And that is where it all begins.

The scent of freshly brewed coffee and the sound of clattering dishes fill my senses as I carefully navigate our conversation. I need to tread lightly, but there are questions that demand answers.

"Katya," I begin, "Don't even try to deny it, I know you stole Whiskey's documents. Why? What were you after?"

"Personal gain," she replies, a touch too quickly. Her eyes dart away for a moment before meeting mine again. "That's all."

"Is it?" I press, leaning forward slightly.

"Look, Mr. Stone," she snaps, her frustration evident. "You don't know anything about me. So don't presume to understand my motives."

"Fair enough," I concede, holding up a hand in surrender.

Her eyes narrow, and I can see the fear flicker behind them. It's time to lay my cards on the table.

"Pipeline bombings, Katya," I say softly, watching her reaction closely. "I believe you're connected to them, why else would you have stolen Whiskey's files."

"Impossible," she hisses, her face flushing with anger. "I only took the documents. I had nothing to do with any bombings."

For a moment, she looks like she might bolt, her eyes darting towards the exit. But then, her expression hardens, and she leans in closer.

"Alright," she says, her voice low and steady. "Let's say, hypothetically, that I am involved. What do you want from me?"

"Truth," I reply simply. "And a chance to let the world know, Ukraine did not blow up the Russian pipelines."

"Truth," she repeats, her eyes clouded with doubt and fear. "That's a dangerous thing in our line of work, Mr. Stone."

"Perhaps," I acknowledge, leaning back in my chair. "But sometimes, it's the only way forward."

As the tension between us lingers and the murmurs of other cafe patrons wash over us, I can't help but wonder if I've pushed too far, too fast. Trust is a fragile thing, especially in this world of espionage. But Katya's silence speaks volumes – I've struck a nerve. And maybe, just maybe, that will be enough to tip the scales in our favor.

A memory flickers in Katya's eyes, haunting and raw. She hesitates, her loyalty to her country at war with the weight of her father's deathbed confession. I watch as she relives that painful moment, her lips moving, recounting the words her father whispered before his final breath.

"Катя, the KGB killed my family," he had confessed, staring up at the sterile hospital ceiling. "Your grandfather was a freedom fighter. After killing my parents and older sister, they took me to an orphanage, brainwashed me into believing communism was our salvation. But I always knew the truth – it was simply a means to survive, for me and then you. After your mother passed away I knew they would recruit you. It broke my heart but I didn't see a way out for me or you but, my darling, you are so strong…"

Katya clenches her fists, her knuckles white with the strain from the burden of her father's secret and I can't help but feel a pang of sympathy for the woman who has been forced to straddle the line between loyalty and betrayal.

"Katya," I say gently, leaning forward in my chair. "Think of the lives at stake here. Russia's actions will only bring more bloodshed, more suffering. You have a chance to make a difference, to change the course of history."

She looks at me, her steely eyes filled with doubt and fear, but there's something else too – a glimmer of hope, perhaps, or maybe just the desperate longing for a reprieve from the darkness that has consumed her world.

"Brian," she whispers, her voice barely audible above the hum of conversation in the cafe. "You don't understand what it's like..."

I reach across the table, my hand hovering just above hers, offering solace without the promise of certainty. "I don't," I admit, my voice steady despite the storm of emotions raging within me.

She studies me for a long moment, as if trying to determine whether I am genuine in my intentions or simply another pawn in the treacherous game of espionage. The silence stretches on, heavy with the weight of unspoken words and uncharted futures.

"Alright," Katya finally says, her voice wavering but resolute. "I'll help you. But you have to promise me one thing."

"Anything."

"Promise me that when this is over, you won't turn me in to the U.S."

"I promise," I reply, sealing our pact with a solemn nod.

~

The sound of the waves crashing against the shore filters through the rustling leaves, a soothing backdrop to the turmoil brewing within me. Katya's eyes, once filled with determination and pride, now glisten with uncertainty as she weighs her options.

"Brian," she starts hesitantly, her voice barely audible, "What if I were to work...on both sides? To become a double agent?"

I look at her, gauging the sincerity in her eyes. It's a dangerous proposition, but one that might just tip the scales in our favor. "It won't be easy," I warn her, my voice low and steady. "You'll be walking a tightrope between two worlds, constantly looking over your shoulder."

Her gaze meets mine, a flicker of fear shadowed by resolve. "I know. But if it can help stop this madness, prevent the suffering of innocent people...then it's a risk I'm willing to take."

"Alright," I say, nodding slowly.

Katya listens intently, her fingers drumming nervously on the table. "But how do we ensure I'm not discovered? The slightest slip-up could cost us everything."

"Trust," I reply, holding her gaze. "Trust in yourself, trust in your instincts, and trust in me. We'll devise a system of communication – codes, dead drops, and encrypted messages to keep our interactions secure."

"Trust," she echoes, her voice thin but determined.

I watch Katya's face as the weight of this settles. She swallows hard, crossing her arms.

"Okay," she says quietly, her voice wavering but resolute. "I'll do it."

"Are you sure?" I ask, my eyebrows knitting together in concern. "This is not a decision to be taken lightly."

"More than anything else in this world," she replies, lifting her gaze to meet mine. Her eyes shine with determination. "My grandfather's memory deserves justice, and I won't let his sacrifice be in vain."

"Good," I say, nodding solemnly. What can you tell me?"

"First, you need to know that the Russians did not blow up their pipelines," she reveals, hesitating for a moment before continuing. "But they have a plan to attack an Israeli pipeline."

"An Israeli pipeline?" I repeat, my mind racing to process the implications. "This could further destabilize the region, and countless lives would be affected."

"Exactly," Katya agrees, her expression grim. "We must uncover the details of their plan and expose it to U.S. intelligence before it's too late."

"Agreed," I say, as I begin to form a strategy. "Here's what we're going to do: you continue your work within their ranks, gathering as much information as possible while maintaining your cover. I'll work on piecing together the puzzle from the outside."

Brian Arrives in Sochi

Katya nods, her lips pressed together. "We'll need a secure method of communication — something they can't trace or intercept."

"Dead drops," I suggest, recalling my days in MI6. "We'll set up designated locations where we can exchange messages without being seen. It's old-school, but it's effective."

"Alright," she agrees. "But we'll need a code — something only the two of us can understand."

"Leave that to me," I say, a sly grin forming on my face. "I've always had a talent for cryptography."

"Brian," Katya says, her voice catching in her throat as she reaches across the table to grasp my hand. "Thank you - for giving me this chance."

"Katya," I reply, gripping her hand tightly. "I have faith in you, and together, we'll find out the details of the Israeli pipeline bombing and halt the world from falling into chaos."

The wind picks up as I begin to leave, the frigid air slicing through my coat like a knife. I glance at Katya, her eyes reflecting the same steely determination that courses through my veins. "Be careful," I warn her, knowing full well the dangers that lie ahead for both of us.

"Same to you, Brian," she responds with a wry smile, her gaze never leaving mine.

With one last nod, we part ways, each stepping into the shadows of our clandestine world, aware that our alliance has forever altered our landscape. I can't help but feel a strange mixture of apprehension and excitement as I start walking towards my safe house, the Sochi night casting its cloak around me.

My footsteps echo off the cobblestone streets, mingling with distant laughter and music from the many bars and restaurants. Though my mind races with questions and doubts, I push them aside to focus on the task at hand – gathering intel, coding messages, and staying one step ahead of the Russian attack on the Israeli pipeline.

As I reach the door of my safe house, I pause, taking one last look at the quiet street behind me. "Can't trust anyone," I mumble under my breath, a constant reminder of the lessons learned during my time in MI6. Yet, here I am, putting my life in the hands of a Russian spy, someone who could betray me in an instant. It's a gamble, but so is everything in this line of work.

My mind races with thoughts of Katya - her resolve wavering between loyalty to her country and the truth her father revealed on his deathbed. Can she really be trusted? Or am I walking into a trap?

Chapter 7
BRIAN AND KATYA IN HAIFA

Over a secure communication link, I video Whiskey and the team back at his Villa, to fill them in on the latest developments.

"Katya's a double agent," I tell the team, watching their eyes widen in surprise. "She's working for us now. She's been instructed to go to Haifa and meet up with a joint team of Hamas and Russians. They're planning to bomb an Israeli pipeline."

"Are you sure about this, Brian?" Whiskey asks, his brow furrowing in concern.

"Positive, she'll be feeding me specific information as the plan unfolds."

"Can we trust her, Brian?" Rosa inquires, her voice filled with skepticism. She knows firsthand the price of misplaced trust.

"Katya's motivations are more complex than they appear." I pause, considering the enigmatic woman who is now my partner in espionage. "But I believe she's on our side. Let's just say she has her own reasons for wanting to see this attack thwarted."

"Alright," Whiskey says. "We'll provide any support you need."

The room is silent for a moment as everyone absorbs this revelation. Then Becca speaks into the computer, her voice determined. "What can we do to help?"

"Keep working your sources, gather what intel you can," I instruct them. "But for now, it's crucial that no one outside this room knows about Katya's true allegiance. We need her to remain undetected."

With that, Brian says his goodbyes and makes preparations for the journey to Haifa. Katya is already there, under order of her Moscow handler, her cover as a Russian translator firmly in place. Brian will pose as a freelance journalist, their paths seemingly crossing by chance.

~

Katya and I arrive in Haifa separately, taking precautions to ensure our covers aren't compromised. The city is a bustling mix of old and new, its streets filled with the sounds and scents of the Mediterranean. It's a beautiful place, but I can't afford to soak it all in. There's work to do.

"Nice to see you again, Mr. Stone," Katya says as she sits down at the next table in a small café near the port. Her tone is friendly but professional, her cold blue eyes scanning the surroundings in a way that only someone trained in the art of espionage would notice.

"Likewise, Miss Rublev," I reply in kind, my senses on high alert. The weight of our mission presses down on me, as does the knowledge that one wrong move could put both our lives at risk.

"Have you made contact with your team?" I ask, taking a sip of coffee.

"Working on it," she says, keeping her voice casual, as though we're discussing the weather. "Shouldn't be long now."

I nod, suddenly struck by the irony of our situation. Here we are, two spies masquerading as ordinary people, engaged in a battle of wits against an enemy who would see us both dead. And yet, despite the danger, there's a part of me invigorated by the challenge of what lies ahead.

"Try the baklava," Katya suggests with a smile, offering me a small piece from her plate. "It's delicious."

"Thanks," I say, accepting the treat and taking a bite, allowing myself a brief moment to savor the sweetness before turning my thoughts back to the task at hand. "There is a place close to the port called, Hanging Bridge at Nesher Park, which features a suspension bridge that crosses a canyon and provides a panoramic view of the city and the port. This park has walking paths, bike lanes, and a visitor center. You can incorporate sight seeing or exercise as a cover for a dead drop. Behind the visitor center there are bathrooms. When you do a drop, place it under the sink in the woman's bathroom. When I need to relay something to you, I will leave a drop there as well. Use this USB", I say sliding it into her pocket.

"Sounds good," she says, taking a moment to scan our surroundings before departing the cafe.

~

Over the next few days, Katya and I exchange intel. I conduct surveillance on key individuals and locations.

"Good work, Katya," I say to myself, one evening as I study the latest batch of intelligence, the weight of Katya's discoveries settling heavily on my shoulders. "We're getting closer to understanding their plan."

As we delve deeper into the intricate web of connections between Hamas and Russia. I spend hours poring over intelligence reports, piecing together the puzzle. It becomes clear this operation is more extensive than initially suspected.

While examining a new map I read Katya's coded message, "Look at these marks – they indicate the locations where Chinese operatives are positioned."

"Fuck, they're really involved," I mutter under my breath, feeling a growing unease as the implications become clearer.

Navigating the precarious world of espionage is a constant game of cat and mouse, with danger lurking around every corner. Katya and I use our skills to avoid detection and gather crucial information, aware that even the slightest misstep could be fatal.

~

I know she's following me, so I go down a winding back alley to a bustling market area. "Here," Katya says suddenly, pulling me into a small, dimly lit shop. The air inside is thick with the scent of spices and incense, making my head swim. "We can blend in with the customers for a moment."

We spend the next several minutes browsing the shelves, our eyes scanning, our ears straining for suspicious sounds. She hands me a small, unmarked envelope, and I can feel the weight of its significance even before I open it.

Russia plans to use a drone loaded with explosives to target the Eilat-Ashkelon pipeline at the junction marked on the map, on March twenty fifth. They'll strike at midnight in three days, during a scheduled maintenance window when security will be lighter. Katya reveals, her eyes betraying the weight of this information.

I stare at the contents of the envelope in disbelief. This information contains evidence of a shocking revelation: a joint operation between Russia and Hamas is underway to sabotage a major oil pipeline in Israel, with the aim of triggering a regional war. The pipeline, known as the Eilat-Ashkelon Pipeline, is a vital link between Israel and Europe, supplying about 40% of Israel's oil needs and generating billions of dollars in revenue.

I quickly scan the contents for more details. According to this, the attack is planned to cause massive damage and fire. The attack would not only cripple Israel's economy and energy security, but also provoke a violent response from Israel, which would likely retaliate against Hamas and its allies in Gaza and Lebanon. This would escalate the already tense situation in the Middle East, and draw the US and its allies into a wider conflict.

But that is not all. Here is proof, that there is a hidden hand behind the attack: China. China has been secretly supporting and financing the operation, as part of its long-term strategy to weaken the US and its influence in the world.

China has two main objectives:

First, to distract and divert the US from its main focus in the Asia-Pacific region, where China is preparing to launch a military invasion of Taiwan, a democratic island that China claims as its own. Taiwan is a key ally of the US and a major producer of semiconductors, the essential components of modern electronics, weapons and AI. By taking over Taiwan, China will gain control over a large part of the world's chip manufacturing, and gain a decisive edge over the US in the global tech race.

Second, to destabilize the global oil market, and increase China's leverage over its energy suppliers and customers. China is the world's largest importer of oil, and relies heavily on the Middle East for its energy needs. By creating chaos and uncertainty in the region, China hopes to secure better deals and terms for its oil imports, and also to undermine the US dollar, which is the dominant currency for oil transactions.

I feel a surge of adrenaline and fear. I realize we stumbled upon a plot that could change the course of history, and put the world on the brink of a new world war. I have to act fast, get this intel to Whiskey so he can alert the U.S. administration.

I quickly stuff the contents back in the envelope, grab Katya by the arm and run out into the busy street. We have to stop the attack, and expose the truth, before it is too late.

"Katya, this is it," I breathe, my heart pounding with a mix of fear and excitement. "This confirms everything we suspected and more, much more."

"Let's get out of here," she says, her eyes darting around the shop, ever vigilant for any signs of danger.

As we slip back into the teeming streets of Haifa, clutching the evidence that could change the course of events and potentially save countless lives, I know that we're not out of the woods yet. We need to get to the airport and back to Mexico.

The sun beats down on us as we make our way through the bustling streets of Haifa, our senses heightened to the danger that surrounds us. Sweat trickles down my back, but it isn't just the heat that's getting to me - it's the constant fear of discovery. Katya and I have already had a few close calls, each one leaving us more on edge than the last.

"Brian," Katya whispers urgently, her eyes darting to a man across the street who seems to be watching us closely. "We're being followed."

"Got it," I reply, careful not to let my voice betray the anxiety tightening in my chest. "Keep moving. We'll lose him in the crowd."

As we weave through the throng of people, I can't help but think about what brought us here: the evidence of China's involvement in this dangerous game. The information we've gathered so far suggests that they've been spying on the U.S., passing crucial intelligence to their Russian allies. And worse still, Steve Stevens, the trusted head of the FBI, is now revealed as a traitor working for China.

"Here," Katya says, pulling me into a taxi cab.

"Go!" I say to the driver.

Turning back to Katya in hushed tone, I say, "there's not much time to stop this attack. We need to get the documents to

Whiskey. He'll have contacts to get this intelligence to the highest levels."

Katya pauses, seemingly lost in thought. Her resourcefulness and intelligence have been invaluable so far, I can't help but wonder where her true allegiances lie. Can I really trust her?

"Perhaps we can set up a secure line through an encrypted messaging service," she suggests. "We can send copies of the details to Whiskey and let him handle getting it to the right people."

"No, there are too many unknowns, this is too important," my gut churns with uncertainty. "We need to ensure it gets to him directly without compromise."

"Agreed," Katya replies. "We should each take separate routes out of Israel, just to be safe."

"Sounds like a plan," I say, though I can't help but feel a twinge of unease at the thought of us separating.

"Brian," Katya says softly, breaking me from my thoughts. "Whatever happens next, just remember we tried our best."

"I hope it's enough, Katya," I reply, touched by her words. "Let's get out of here."

With our preparations complete, we part ways, each taking a different route out of Israel. Though we leave separately, I know that our joint mission to foil Russia's plan and expose China's involvement has only just begun. The fight for global security is far from over.

~

As I make my way through the dimly lit streets of Haifa, my thoughts drift to Whiskey, the charismatic leader who brings people together, even in the darkest of times. I know that once he receives the information we've gathered, he'll do everything in his power to bring this plot to light and protect innocent lives. Trusting him has never been an issue for me, but now with China's involvement and a traitor among us, I find myself questioning everything.

"Stop overthinking it, Brian," I mutter to myself, shaking off the growing paranoia. "Focus on the mission."

I continue navigating the labyrinthine streets, pausing every now and then to ensure I'm not being followed. My years as an ex-MI6 agent have honed my instincts, and I rely on them to keep me from harm.

"Almost there," I whisper, pushing onward. My heart beats faster, adrenaline coursing through my veins. This isn't just about a pipeline attack anymore — it's about global security, and the fight against those who seek to disrupt it.

Finally, I reach the airport, my eyes scanning the area for any signs of trouble. Relief washes over me when I spot Katya inside at a check in desk. I feel a renewed sense of determination.

Chapter 8
NATALIE IS MISSING

I enjoy the coolness of Cantina Habaneros in Puerto Morelos, away from the sun's heat. It's a relaxed afternoon, and I drink my chilled beer and chat with some of the guys, taking a breather from the investigation. Brian and Katya in Israel are collecting intel and making great progress.

"Whiskey," says Frank, an old friend from Texas, "Did you see the Stars' Goalie take that slap shot to the head?"

"Man that looked painful, I hope he's alright."

Just then, Sarah, a close friend of Natalie's, rushes over, her blonde hair tangled by the wind. "Whiskey, have you seen Natalie today? She hasn't been answering her phone and she's not home."

"I haven't seen her, Sarah but I'll check with Nikos and Hugo at Barracuda, they're her usual buddies every night."

My friends nod, and we quickly split up to canvass the area.

"Hey, Whiskey!" shouts Frank, as he trots over with a concerned expression. "I just talked to Tomas. He said he saw Natalie heading into the mangroves yesterday. Alone."

"Damn." The mangroves are a dense, tangled mess of roots, branches and swamps that can be disorienting for even the most experienced adventurer. Not to mention it's home to crocodiles. "All right, we're gonna need more help to search those mangroves. But we gotta keep it quiet; don't want to cause a panic."

"Understood, Whiskey," Frank replies, nodding.

I call the rest of our little group of expats and we organize ourselves into a search party. As we set off towards the mangroves, I feel a knot tighten in my gut.

"Natalie," I think to myself. "Why would you go in to the mangroves."

The sun beats down relentlessly on the mangroves as we push deeper into their tangled maze, sweat dripping from our brows. Mosquitoes buzz around us, but none of us bother to swat them. We're too focused, too worried about Natalie.

"Spread out, but stay within earshot," I instruct my friends. "We don't need anyone else getting lost in here."

"Understood," they echo, fanning out as we trudge onward. The gnarled roots and twisted branches seem to close in around me, suffocating, as if trying to force me back.

"Damn it, where are you, Natalie?" I mutter under my breath, frustration boiling over. My head aches with worry, and I can't help but wonder if she's even still alive.

"Whiskey!" Sarah, calls out abruptly. Her voice is shaky, urgent. "Over here!"

I rush towards her, heart hammering in my chest. As I approach, I see the look of horror on Sarah's face, and suddenly, I'm afraid to see what she's found. But I steel myself and force my legs to carry me forward.

"Geezus," I whisper, my voice barely audible through the lump in my throat. "Move back slowly Sarah."

Moving slowly backward my eyes stay focused on the seemingly asleep crocodile, sprawled across the damp ground, basking in the sun.

"Whiskey," Sarah murmurs, her voice trembling. "What do we do now?

"Call everyone back," I say, forcing myself to keep an eye on the crocodile and alert for any others in the area.

"Right," she agrees, her voice choked with fear. She turns away to call the others. I curse under my breath, keeping an eye on the croc.

Once out of the mangrove, my friends gather around me, their faces pale and drawn, I can see the same questions reflected in their eyes. And deep down, a cold fear takes root in my heart: that if Natalie came into the mangroves, she likely didn't make it out.

"Whiskey?" Josh asks hesitantly, breaking the silence. "What now?"

"Listen up, folks," I say, turning to face my friends who are waiting for instructions. "I need you to fan out and gather any information you can about Natalie's recent activities and contacts.

"I'll call the authorities and report her missing. I'm headed to Barracuda, to talk to Nikos and Hugo. Let's meet at Habaneros in an hour."

"Agreed," my friends murmur, their voices low but resolute.

~

I'm trying to piece together the puzzle that is Natalie's disappearance. My mind races back and forth between the Russians and her husband's military involvement in Iran.

"Whiskey, my friend, what brings you here this time of day?" Nikos asks, as I enter Barracuda.

"It's Natalie, she's missing. When is the last time you saw her?"

"Bhah, I'm sure she's not missing Whiskey. Maybe she hooked up with someone. I saw her chatting and dancing with some tourists here night before last."

"Yeah you might be right but Sarah is very concerned. No one has seen or heard from her in a couple days. She's not answering her phone and she's not home."

"I'll ask around Whiskey but I wouldn't worry about it. I'm sure she's fine. This town is very safe."

"Thanks Nikos."

~

I stand in the entrance of Natalie's apartment, scanning the room for anything that might shed light on her disappearance.

The place seems normal, except for a few bikinis and towels thrown over the sofa, not a thing is out of place. I can't shake the feeling that this is all connected to the Russians or her husband's involvement in Iran.

My eyes dart around the room, searching for anything out of the ordinary. That's when I notice her handbag, holding it up I notice the seams slightly uneven near the bottom. Could it be? My fingers trace the edges, locating a hidden zipper. I pull it open slowly, revealing a hidden compartment.

"Son of a gun," I whisper, my suspicions growing stronger. Inside is a piece of paper with my name and a photocopy of my drivers license photo.

"Who are you Natalie?" my heart pounding in my chest. "And what is going on here?"

My heart clenches in my chest as I pull out my phone, desperately trying to reach Brian and Katya. They need to get back here, now. The phone rings and rings, but there's no answer. Damn it.

"Pick up, pick up," I mutter under my breath, frustration mounting with each unanswered ring. Finally, Brian's voicemail greets me, and I leave an urgent message. "Brian, Katya, it's Whiskey. Something's happened. It's about Natalie. Get back to Puerto Morelos as soon as you can."

Chapter 9
THE CARTEL CONNECTION

Whiskey leaned against veranda, gazing out at the shimmering turquoise waters that stretched as far as the eye could see. The breeze brought back memories of Natalie's laughter and her carefree spirit... before she vanished without a trace.

"Rosa," I say, turning my gaze indoors. "We need to talk."

"About what?" She replies coolly, setting the glass down.

"About Natalie. And about the Cartel." I let the words hang in the air for a moment, watching her face for any sign of reaction. "I think we need their help."

Rosa hesitates, her dark eyes narrowing as she weighs the implications of what I'm suggesting. I can tell she doesn't like the idea, not one bit, but I also know that she'd do anything to protect her friends. Even if it means reaching out to the one group of people she swore never to get involved with again.

"Whiskey... you know what they're capable of. You sure you want to go down this road?"

"Look, I'm not exactly thrilled about it either, but we're running out of options here, and we have no leads on where Natalie might be. If anyone knows something it's them."

She bites her lip, clearly torn between her loyalty to her friends and her fear of the consequences that might come from contacting the Cartel. For a moment, I wonder if she'll refuse outright, but then she looks me in the eyes and nods.

"Alright," she says quietly. "I'll do it. But we have to be careful, Whiskey. If word gets out that we're talking to them... well, you know what could happen."

"Trust me, darling, I know all too well. I also know that we're not going to find Natalie on our own. And we need to know if the Russians are involved. We need their help, whether we like it or not."

Rosa nods once more, her expression set with determination. "I'll make some calls, see what I can dig up. Discreetly."

"Thank you, Rosa, you're a good friend."

"Let's just hope this doesn't come back to bite us, Whiskey," she replies, her gaze lingering on the horizon for a moment before she turns away, picking up her phone and dialing a number she swore she'd never use again.

~

A couple of days later, I find myself sitting in a dimly lit cantina in La Colonia, with Rosa, waiting for her contact to arrive. We've been nursing our cervezas for what feels like an eternity. Rosa's eyes dart around nervously, her fingers tapping a restless rhythm on the table.

"Relax, Rosa'," I tell her, trying to sound more confident than I feel. "We're gonna get the information we need, and then we'll be out of here."

"Easy for you to say," she mutters under her breath.

Finally, a tall, imposing man walks in, his dark jeans and stetson standing out among the casual tropical attire of the other patrons. He scans the room before making his way towards us. As he sits down, Rosa gives me a reassuring squeeze on the arm.

"Whiskey, this is Hector. Hector, Whiskey," she introduces us, her voice barely above a whisper.

"Nice to meet you, Hector," I say, extending my hand. He takes it, his grip firm and unyielding.

"Let's get straight to the point," Hector says, his voice low and gravelly. "Rosa tells me you're looking for information about a Russian hitman. What do you want to know?"

I take a deep breath, steeling myself for the conversation ahead. "We need to know if there is a Russian hitman around, if so, he might have something to do with the disappearance of our friend, Natalie. We're hoping you might have some intel on anyone matching that description."

Hector regards me coldly for a moment before answering. "There is someone who might fit the bill. His name is Nikos. We heard whispers he used to be an enforcer for the Russian mafia in New York City, before coming to Puerto Morelos. As you probably know he is the big Greek bartender at Barracuda. He appears to be just that though, a bartender."

Rosa and I exchange a glance, my suspicions about Nikos past now seeming more plausible than ever. "Thank you, Hector," Rosa says, her voice shaking slightly.

"Be careful," Hector warns as he stands to leave.

As he slips out the door, Rosa and I sit in silence, processing the new information about Nikos. Our loyalties are being tested now more than ever, and I can't help but wonder how deep the web of betrayal extends in this treacherous world of espionage. For now, though, we have a lead to follow, and perhaps a chance to find Natalie before it's too late.

~

As the sun lowers in the sky casting shadows over the dusty streets of La Colonia, Rosa and I sit alone at the small table in the cantina, sipping on cold cervezas as we wrestle with what Hector told us about Nikos.

"Whiskey," Rosa begins, her voice low and cautious, "I know we can't ignore this information, but are we really going to turn on one of our own without any solid proof?"

I take a swig of my beer, feeling the condensation drip down onto my sun-weathered hand. "Rosa, you know as well as I do that in this game, it's better to be safe than sorry. If there's even a chance that Nikos is involved with Natalie's disappearance, we've got to find out for sure."

Rosa runs a hand through her dark hair, frustration creasing her brow. "But what if we're wrong? What if he's innocent and we destroy our friendship over nothing?"

"Then we'll apologize, mend fences, and move on." I reply, shrugging my shoulders. "But if we're right, and he's mixed up in something dangerous, we need to know."

A heavy silence falls between us, interrupted only by the distant sounds of laughter and mariachi music drifting through the warm evening air. I can tell Rosa's struggling with the decision to confront Nikos.

"Alright," she finally says, her voice firm and resolute. "Let's talk to Nikos."

"Ok," I nod, draining the last of my beer. "Now let's go to Barracuda."

We get in the car with Agent Santiago, and drive back to Puerto Morelos Beachside from La Colonia, along the only road that cuts through the mangroves. Nikos is behind the bar as always. He welcomes us with a wide grin, oblivious to the trouble that's looming under the radar.

"Whiskey! Rosa!" He exclaims, as he passes over two shots of tequila. "What brings you by this early in the evening?"

I catch Rosa's eye, and she gives me a slight nod, signaling that it's time to confront our friend. My gut churns with unease, but I know it's something I have to do.

"Actually, Nikos, we need to talk to you about something important. Something that could affect all of us."

Nikos' smile falters, and he leans in closer, his eyes searching mine for answers. "What's going on, Whiskey?"

"Rosa and I have been looking into Natalie's disappearance," I begin, feeling the weight of the words as they leave my lips. "And we've heard some things about your past, about your connections to the Russian mafia. We need you to be honest with us, Nikos. Are you mixed up in something dangerous?"

The dim lighting in the bar seems to grow darker as I watch Nikos' face harden. His eyes narrow, brows furrowing in suspicion.

"Whiskey, I don't know what you're talking about," he says, his voice low and steady. "I have no connections to any Russians."

"Come on, Nikos," Rosa chimes in gently. "We just want to help. But we can't do that unless you're honest with us."

Nikos looks from her to me, a mixture of anger and hurt in his eyes. But something in his expression shifts, like a shutter being drawn back, revealing a glimpse of the truth behind his carefully constructed facade.

"Alright," he sighs, looking down at the worn wooden bar-top. "I was an enforcer for the Russian mafia in New York City — but that was a long time ago. I left that life behind when I came here to Puerto Morelos."

My heart thuds against my ribcage as I process this revelation. The man I've come to know and trust over these past few years turns out to be a former member of the Russian mob. But despite the shock, I can't help but feel a surge of empathy for him.

"Damn, Nikos, why didn't you tell us?" I ask, trying to keep my tone even.

"Whiskey, I'm not involved with them anymore," he protests, meeting my gaze with intensity. "I came here to start fresh, to leave that darkness behind. You and the people of this town, you've become my family. I'd never do anything to put you in danger."

His words hang heavy in the stale air of the bar, and I can see the raw honesty in his eyes. But trust is a fragile thing, and once it's broken, it's not easy to repair.

"Listen, Nikos, I want to believe you, I really do. But there's a lot at stake here, You understand that, don't you?"

Nikos nods slowly, "I understand."

When I look into his eyes — those dark pools that hold a lifetime of secrets — I find myself wanting to believe him.

"Alright," I say finally, clapping him on the shoulder. "Nikos: if your past ever comes knocking, you don't hesitate to tell me.

~

The moon rises casting glimmering light on the sea. I gather our group on the terrace. I can feel the weight of my words as I prepare to let them in on the secret — that our friend Nikos has a past darker than any of us ever imagined.

Clearing my throat and meeting each set of eyes in turn. "We've got some news about Nikos."

A hush settles over the group like a shroud, and I see fear flicker in their gazes. Rosa stands by my side, her hand resting gently on my arm, offering support and reassurance.

"Turns out, our man Nikos used to be an enforcer for the Russian mob back in New York City."

"Fuck," Josh mutters, his eyes widening as he takes in the implications.

"Whiskey, are you sure about this?" asks Karlie, disbelief etching lines into her face.

"I'm sure, Rosa and I just spoke with him. He says he's no longer connected and left that life behind long ago. We're choosing to trust him."

"Trust him?" Bob scoffs, his brow furrowed in anger. "Whiskey, do you have any idea what kind of danger we're in now? This isn't just a game, man!"

"Easy, Bob," Rosa interjects, her voice calm but firm. "We understand the risks. But we also know that Nikos has been a good friend for years. He's like family."

I nod in agreement, "He's one of us. Besides, we've got bigger fish to fry. We still have to find Natalie and figure out who's behind this whole mess in Israel before it blows up in our faces."

"Whiskey's right," says Rosa, her eyes burning with determination. "We need to focus on the task at hand and stay vigilant."

"Fuck." Josh says finally, his voice subdued but resolute. "We'll stand by Nikos, despite his past. But if anything goes wrong, if any of us gets hurt because of his connections..."

"Then we'll deal with it," I interrupt, cutting him off before he can finish his threat. "Together, like we always have."

And with that, we clear out, a motley crew of expats turned spies, ready to face whatever danger awaits us in the shadows.

Chapter 10
BRIAN AND KATYA BACK IN MEXICO

The moment my feet hit the ground in Cancun, I can feel the humidity clinging to my skin. The air is thick with it, and despite the unease settling in my gut, I find some small comfort in the familiar sensation. Katya is inside, waiting for me.

"Call Whiskey," she says, her eyes scanning our surroundings for any sign of danger. "We need a private car."

"Already on it," I reply, pulling out my burner phone and dialing the number. After a few rings, Whiskey's voice comes through the line.

"Brian! You made it alright?"

"Safe and sound, Whiskey," I assure him. "We are at Cancun airport, could use a car. We want to avoid any potential surveillance here."

"Sure thing, it'll be there in thirty minutes. Look for a tall bulky man dressed in black with a black sedan. I'm sure he'll stand out."

"Thanks, Whiskey." I hang up, and we make our way to the designated pickup spot, both of us hyper-aware of our surroundings.

As the black sedan pulls up, I glance over at Katya. She's got this steely glint in her eye that tells me she's prepared for anything. It's part of what makes her such a formidable spy, and I'd be lying if I said it didn't impress the hell out of me.

"Ready?" I ask, opening the door for her.

"Always," she replies, sliding into the backseat with a grace that's almost feline. I follow suit, closing the door behind me as the driver speeds off towards Puerto Morelos.

"Alright," I say, turning to face Katya. "Let's go over the details. We need to be absolutely certain of what we're presenting to Whiskey and the others."

"Agreed," she nods, her expression serious. "The Russians and Hamas plan to bomb the Israeli pipeline on March twenty fifth, midnight in two days. China is backing the whole mission to draw the U.S. further into the conflict of the Mideast. Thus weakening the U.S. military's ability to respond, when China takes over Taiwan. That's the highlights?"

"Right," I confirm, my mind racing with the implications of this attack. "We also have evidence that Steve Stevens, the man we thought was a trustworthy ally, is actually a traitor working for China."

"Yes," Katya says. "We need to make sure Whiskey understands the gravity of the situation. There's no time for hesitation or second-guessing."

"True, it's not just about stopping an attack — it's about exposing the rot at the heart of our own government."

Katya's eyes meet mine, filled with a fierce determination that matches my own. Together, we're going to bring this whole twisted web of lies and deceit crashing down.

"Let's do this," I say firmly.

"Yes," she replies, her gaze never wavering. "Da."

~

Salt fills the air as we pull into the quiet coastal town of Puerto Morelos. My eyes dart around, taking in every detail, searching for anything out of place. I glance over at Katya, who's doing the same.

"Brian," she whispers, her voice tense. "Look, there's a black SUV parked near Whiskey's villa. It doesn't seem to belong here."

"Fuck." I mutter, my heart pounding. "We might not have shaken them after all."

Before I can say another word, the driver speaks up. "Don't worry about that vehicle, it's Agent Santiago's team. They're on your side."

I exhale a sigh of relief, grateful that we have allies in this treacherous game of espionage. We park the car and quickly make our way inside the villa. The door creaks open, revealing Whiskey, his lined face creased with anxiety. Our fellow expats are gathered around him, their expressions a mix of concern and resolve.

"Brian, Katya," Whiskey says gruffly, giving them both a hug. "Thank God you made it back in one piece."

"Whiskey," I reply, "we have urgent important information to share."

"Let's get straight to it," he says, motioning for us to sit down. I look around the room, taking in the faces of these brave men and women who have chosen to stand with us against the forces of chaos and destruction.

"Nice to see you all," I begin, glancing at Katya for support. "As you know we've discovered evidence of a Russian plan to bomb an Israeli pipeline. We know the details. This attack is imminent, and we need to act fast to prevent catastrophe."

Whiskey's eyes narrow. "We can't let them succeed."

"Furthermore," I add, "Steve Stevens, a man we thought was an ally, is actually a traitor working for China."

A gasp of disbelief ripples through the room, but it's quickly replaced by a grim determination. Whiskey takes a deep breath, his face set with resolve.

"Then we have no time to lose," he says, looking around the room at each of his friends. "We need to get this evidence to the President himself."

The room quickly fills with the sounds of urgent phone calls and fingers tapping on keyboards as we all try to find the best way to reach the president. I can feel the tension in the air, like a noose tightening around our necks. Everyone is aware of what's at stake, but nobody's backing down.

"Shoot," Karlie mutters under her breath when she hits another dead end. She's trying to track down someone who can get us a direct line to the president, but it seems like every connection is being blocked or redirected.

"I just remembered something," Josh says, his voice tense. "It's not a direct line, but it's close. A high-ranking official in the State Department owes me a favor."

"Call them," Whiskey orders, his jaw tight.

"Already on it," Josh replies, dialing the number.

As he talks in hushed tones, everyone in the room holds their breath, waiting to see if this will be our breakthrough. The tension is so thick, you could cut it with a knife. I can't shake the image of Steve's smug face from my mind – how he must have thought I was just an old fool.

"Okay, we're in," Josh finally announces, hanging up the phone. "They'll get our message to the White House within the hour."

"Good work," Whiskey says, clapping him on the back. "Now let's get that evidence ready to send. We don't have a moment to lose."

~

As the final pieces of evidence are bundled together and sent off, I feel a small measure of relief wash over me. The stakes have never been higher, and we've just taken a leap of faith, trusting that our actions will make a difference.

"Thank you, Whiskey," Katya says, her voice cracking with emotion. "And thank all of you. Thank you for trusting me."

Brian adds, "You are like family to us now, and we'll never forget what you've done here."

Whiskey's stern demeanour softens, and he nods. "We're all in this together," he replies. "Now let's get some ice-cold beers - we've earned it."

As we head out to the terrace, laughter and good-natured ribbing fill the air, breaking through the lingering tension. I marvel at the camaraderie among this crew of expats, each with their own unique history but bound together by a friendship formed in a little slice of paradise.

I crack open a beer, letting the cold liquid slide down my throat as I lean against the railing and look out at the ocean. It's beautiful, almost a cruel reminder of all we have to lose, as we teeter on the brink of disaster.

"Brian," I say, turning to him, "do you think we did enough?"

He pauses for a moment, studying the waves washing against the shore. "I don't know," he admits. "But we did everything we could, and that's all anyone can ask of us."

I nod, knowing he's right. We played our part, and now it's up to others to carry the torch. All we can do is hope that our efforts are not in vain.

"Cheers," I say, raising my beer in a toast to our accomplishment.

"Cheers," he echoes, clinking his bottle against mine. Turning to the others he says, "Hey, who's up for dinner at La Sirena? Whiskey's buying."

Laughter breaks out and in unison everyone yells, "hell yeah!"

~

All the intel managed to reach the Pentagon. Director Burns, and a team of senior officials from the CIA, the NSA, the DOD, and the White House. He quickly briefs them on the situation, and shows them the evidence. The room is filled with shock and disbelief, as the officials realize the gravity and urgency of the threat.

"We have to act now," Burns says. "We can't let China get away with this. They are playing with fire, and they are putting the world at risk. We have two main objectives: to stop the attack on Israel, and to defend Taiwan from China's invasion. We have to coordinate with our allies and partners, and use all the resources and capabilities we have. The Secretary of Defence, General MacFadgen, will now brief you further."

"Thank you Director Burns," starts the General. "For Israel, we have to warn them and share the intelligence we have. We also have to work with the Mossad and other agencies to identify and neutralize the operatives and the explosives. We have to prevent the attack from happening, or at least minimize the damage and the fallout."

"For Taiwan, we have to increase our military presence and readiness in the region. We have to deploy more ships, aircraft, and troops to bases and allies near Taiwan, such as Japan, South Korea, and the Philippines. We have to conduct joint exercises and patrols, and enhance our missile defense and cyber capabilities. This could deter or delay China's attack, reassure Taiwan and other partners, and prepare for a potential response."

"We also have to provide direct or indirect assistance to Taiwan's defense. We have to supply them with weapons, intelligence, logistics, and training. We have to send military advisers or special forces, if necessary. We have to help them resist or repel China's invasion.

The officials nod in agreement, and begin to make phone calls and issue orders. They know they have little time to waste, and they have to act fast and decisively. They also know they are facing a formidable adversary, and they have to be prepared for the worst. They hope their actions will prevent a catastrophe, and preserve the peace and stability of the world.

Chapter 11
WHO IS NATALIE?

The palms sway and swish casting shadows under the palapa at La Sirena. My friends and I are relaxing, sipping various cocktail concoctions. The conversation turns to one subject we can't avoid: Natalie's sudden disappearance.

"It's been three weeks since anyone has seen Natalie. Katya, I have to ask, do you know anything about Natalie's disappearance, do you think the Russians got to her?" I ask.

"Whiskey," Rosa says, her dark eyes narrowing, "you know how it is down here. People come and go all the time. Maybe she just moved on."

I shake my head, unable to accept that. "No, not Natalie. She was waiting for her husband to come back from Iran. She wouldn't up and leave like that without even packing."

"Whiskey's right," Bob chimes in, his thin lips pressed into a tight line. "Natalie always seemed so... scared. Like she knew someone was watching her. I mean, hell, I'd be paranoid too if I were involved with those Russian types... sorry Katya."

"Exactly, and what if her husband's military involvement in Iran has something to do with this whole mess? Are they using her to get to him? And why does she have my photo? Katya can you help us out!" I snap, frustration getting the better of me.

Beside me, Katya shifts in her seat.

"Whiskey, there is something you need to know about Natalie," she says, her voice soft yet firm. "She isn't who you think she is."

"Really?" I ask, my brows furrowed. "And how exactly would you know that?"

"Because," she hesitates for a moment, searching for the right words. "Natalie's not a military wife waiting for her husband. She is an ex-stripper. From Vegas."

"Wait, what?" Brian interjects, his face a mix of confusion and disbelief. "Are you telling us she came here to steal the documents from Whiskey?"

"Yes," Katya nods solemnly. "That was her mission."

"Katya," I say, trying to keep my voice steady. "Tell us everything you know. What was her plan? Why did she fail? Where could she be?"

"Her plan was simple," she explains, her words measured and deliberate. "A Russian oligarch sent her here to infiltrate your life, gain your trust, and steal the documents. But she didn't expect one thing: to fall for you, Whiskey."

"Fall for me?" I scoff, shaking my head. "How do you even know this?"

Who is Natalie?

"I have my sources," she replies, her expression unreadable. "Natalie was supposed to complete her mission and leave, but she couldn't. She cared too much about you, and that's why she failed."

The weight of her revelation sinks in, as I reckon with the fact that Natalie wasn't who I thought she was. But, if what Katya's saying is true, then she's still in danger, caught between her mission and her feelings for me. And now, more than ever, I need to find her before it's too late.

"Who's pulling her strings, then? Who's this Russian oligarch you're talking about?"

Katya hesitates for a moment before answering. "His name is Viktor Romanov. A ruthless man with far-reaching influence. Natalie met him in Vegas when she was still dancing. He was a client of hers, and he saw an opportunity to use her."

"Fuck" Brian mutters, running his fingers through his hair.

"Viktor could be very persuasive," Katya continues. "He convinced Natalie that he loved her, and that by carrying out this mission, they could be together. But it was all lies — just another way for him to manipulate her."

I can't help but feel a pang of empathy for Natalie, as I imagine her caught in the web of Viktor's deceit.

"Whiskey," Katya says softly, sensing my turmoil. "I know this is hard for you, but please understand that Natalie didn't want to hurt you. She was trapped, and Viktor made sure she had no way out. Which is why we need to find her before Viktor does. If he hasn't already."

As much as I hate to admit it, Katya's right. No matter what kind of person Natalie turned out to be, she's still in danger, and it's up to us to save her. "Alright," I say finally, my resolve building. "Let's find Natalie, and bring her home."

~

I glance around the table at my friends, their faces a mix deep concern and fear for Natalie. The weight of Natalie's betrayal hangs heavy in the air, but we all know that finding her is our top priority now. She's in danger, and no matter what she's done, we can't just leave her to whatever fate awaits her.

"We need to figure out where Natalie could be. Does anyone have any ideas?"

"Maybe she's hiding out somewhere in town," responds Rosa.

"Then we need to check every damn inch of this town," I declare, feeling a surge of determination. "First thing tomorrow, Brian and Rosa, you take La Colonia, Josh and Karlie, you take the square and surrounding area, Bob and Becca, you go to the beach bars, and Katya and I will take the north, residential area."

"Whiskey, I think we should also consider the fact that she may not even be alive," Josh says somberly, casting a worried glance in my direction.

"Damn it, Josh," I grit my teeth, my fists balling up in anger. "I can't accept that. Not until we've searched everywhere."

"Easy, Whiskey," Josh raises his hands defensively. "I'm just sayin' we need to be prepared for the worst."

"I know," I sigh, he's right. "But let's focus on finding her first. We'll deal with the rest when we get there."

Who is Natalie?

I can't help but feel both hopeful and terrified. The thought of losing Natalie — even after everything she's done — is unbearable.

~

Back at my Villa, after a day of searching, and coming up with nothing. We feel deflated. My brain is turning and I know, "We're missing something, some piece of the puzzle."

"Whiskey, what about Nikos?" Becca suggests, her eyes wide with urgency. "He's got connections and he might have heard something new."

"Good idea." I dial Nikos's number and hold the phone to my ear, pacing back and forth as it rings. My mind races with possibilities, each more terrifying than the last.

"Whiskey?" Nikos answers, his deep voice crackling through the speaker.

"Hey, Nikos. We need your help. We are certain Natalie's in trouble, she's mixed up with some dangerous people."

"What do you need, Whiskey?"

"Information, Nikos. Anything you've heard about Russians in town or any leads on where Natalie could be."

"Let's talk Whiskey. Can you come to the bar?" he replies.

"I'll be there in ten minutes." I say before ending the call, feeling a small glimmer of hope.

"Alright, everyone. It seems Nikos has some information he wants to share with us. I'm headed to Barracuda now. Josh - Brian - you coming?"

"Of course, Whiskey," they reply.

Chapter 12
NIKOS CONFESSION

The moon's a spotlight on the gravel as I lead Brian and Josh through the dark alley behind the bar.

"Whiskey, you sure Nikos said to meet back here?" Brian mutters, his eyes darting to each shadow we pass.

"That's what he said."

As if on cue, a hulking figure steps out from behind a dumpster, startling the hell out of Josh. I stifle a chuckle at the sight of the usually unflappable hedge fund manager flinching.

"Fuck, Nikos," Josh says, recovering quickly. "You got a real talent for theatrics, don't you?"

"Comes with the territory," Nikos replies, his thick Greek accent rumbling like distant thunder. The man's a damn mountain, but his loyalty runs deeper than any roots. We've all got secrets, and I reckon Nikos has more than most.

"Alright, let's not waste time," Brian cuts in, his impatience itching at him like an old scar. "Nikos, what do you know about Natalie's disappearance?"

Nikos looks at each of us in turn, his eyes weighed down by some invisible burden. I can see the conflict within him, fighting between his instincts to protect and his loyalty to his friends.

"Fine," he sighs finally. "I helped her escape."

"Escape?" I ask, taken aback. "From what?"

"From them," Nikos whispers. "The Russians."

"Son of a bitch," Josh curses under his breath, the gravity of the situation sinking in like a stone dropped into water.

Nikos nods, his face grim. "She never meant to be a spy, but they targeted her. They knew she was vulnerable, alone."

"Why didn't you tell me? Is she safe? Where is she now?" I ask.

"Whiskey," Brian says, placing a hand on my shoulder. "Let Nikos explain."

I nod, forcing myself to take a deep breath. This isn't the time for rash decisions or impulsive actions.

"Alright, talk," I say to Nikos, my voice steady. "Tell us everything."

"First of all, you should know that Natalie is safe," Nikos begins, his words measured and deliberate. "I made sure of that. She's currently in Byron Bay, Australia."

"Byron Bay?" Josh asks, the relief in his eyes unmistakable.

"Smart move," Brian nods, his brow furrowing in thought. "It's remote, yet still has a strong expat community. She should be able to blend in well there."

"Thank God she's safe," I say, feeling the weight on my chest ease just a little. "But why did the Russians target her?"

Nikos hesitates for a moment, glancing at the ground as if gathering his thoughts. "I think it's best if I start at the beginning. You see, Natalie didn't have the easiest upbringing. Her mother was a stripper, got knocked up, and Natalie never knew her father."

"Damn," I mutter, trying to wrap my head around the information. "That must've been tough on her."

"Sure was," Nikos agrees, rubbing the back of his neck. "She grew up fast, always looking out for herself and her mom. But when her mother passed away, it left her more vulnerable than ever."

"Is that why the Russians targeted her?" Brian asks, his expression darkening with concern.

"Partly," Nikos admits. "They knew she had no one to watch her back, no family to raise hell if she went missing. But there was something else, something that made her even more valuable to them."

As he speaks, I can sense the urgency in his words, the desperate need to make us understand the gravity of the situation. Trust and betrayal, they weave together like the threads of some twisted tapestry, and we're all caught up in it, whether we like it or not.

"Whatever it is," I say firmly, "we'll make sure Natalie stays safe."

"Thank you, Whiskey," Nikos replies with a genuine smile. "I knew I could count on you. On all of you."

"Of course," Brian adds.

The dim glow of a streetlamp casts long shadows across the alley, creating an eerie sense of isolation. A chill runs down my spine as Nikos continues his story.

"Her mother... she OD'd when Natalie was only 14," he says, remorse etched on his face. "Natalie found her body lying cold and lifeless on their apartment floor."

I can almost see the scene in my mind — a young girl, hardened by circumstance but still innocent at heart, discovering the ultimate betrayal of death. It makes me sick to think about it.

"That's rough," Josh mutters, rubbing the back of his neck.

"Rough" doesn't even begin to cover it. In that moment, I feel a fierce protectiveness for Natalie surge within me. The girl's been through hell, and now we need to make sure no one drags her back into it.

"Her mother's death left her vulnerable," Nikos continues, his eyes fixed on some unseen point in the distance. "No family, no friends, just a kid trying to survive in a cruel world."

"That's why the Russians targeted her," says Brian, his brow furrowed with worry.

"Exactly," Nikos replies, his voice heavy with emotion. "They prey on the weak, those who have nothing and no one to protect them. They knew she'd be easy to manipulate, to control."

A bitter taste fills my mouth. The thought of how easily Natalie was ensnared by these monsters disgusts me. She deserved so much better than this.

"Those bastards," I curse under my breath. "We will keep Natalie safe – no matter what it takes.

"Speaking of which, how did you manage to get her out?" I inquire, genuinely curious.

"Let's just say I still have some contacts from my past life," Nikos replies with a cryptic smile. "And they owed me a favor."

"Whatever you did, we're grateful," Josh says earnestly, echoing my own thoughts. "You risked your neck for her, Nikos. That means a lot."

"Friends take care of each other," Nikos states simply, but there's a depth of emotion behind his words.

"Are you sure she's safe?" I ask, my voice tense with worry. "I mean, really safe?"

"Trust me," Nikos reassures us, his dark eyes filled with sincerity. "Natalie is far away from the Russian oligarch and his goons. They won't find her in Byron Bay."

The wind picks up, howling through the alley as if it knows the secrets we've just shared. I shiver, pulling my jacket tighter around me. "Now that we know where Natalie is and that she's safe," I say, shifting my gaze from one friend to another, "we need to make damn sure it stays that way. The Russians can't find her."

"Absolutely," Brian affirms, the steely determination in his voice matching the sharp glint in his eyes. "We keep her location a secret, even amongst ourselves. Loose lips sink ships, as they say. And in this case, loose lips could very well cost Natalie her life."

Chapter 13
CONFRONTING STEVE STEVENS

Whiskey's fingers tremble slightly as he types in the encryption code, setting up a secure video chat with Steve Stevens. The sun streams in through the open window of his Puerto Morelos Villa, warming his wrinkled skin and casting long shadows on the floor.

The call connects, and I wait for Steve to join. Memories of our days in the oil industry together flood my mind, followed by darker thoughts of deception and betrayal. How could someone I once trusted be involved with the Russians?

"Think, Whiskey," I tell myself, trying to remember if there were any signs of Steve's duplicity. "You're good at reading people." But Steve had always been a tough nut to crack – no-nonsense, professional, yet somehow always distant.

As the seconds tick by, my heart rate increases, and I become acutely aware of the sweat forming on my forehead. My thoughts are a whirlwind: What if Steve has already sold us out to the enemy? What if he's playing both sides? What if he's behind all this mess?

"Focus," I admonish myself, taking a deep breath. "Don't jump to conclusions."

Suddenly, Steve's face appears on the screen, his hawk-like eyes betraying a tension I've rarely seen in him. He offers a tight-lipped smile that doesn't reach his eyes, confirming my gut feeling that something is amiss.

"Whiskey," he says, his voice strained, "what's up?"

I take a deep breath, steeling myself for the confrontation that's about to unfold. My heart pounds against my ribs, but I manage to keep my voice steady.

"You tell me Steve," I reply, forcing a casual tone. "I've got to ask you something, and I need you to be straight with me."

He squints at the screen, his brow furrowed in suspicion. "Alright," he says cautiously, "what's on your mind?"

"Been hearing things, Steve," I begin, my words slow and deliberate. "Things I don't want to believe, but can't ignore. I need to know: what's going on between you, the Russians and the Chinese?"

His eyes widen slightly, and he opens his mouth to speak, but no words come out. For a moment, all I can hear is the distant swish of the palm leaves outside my window and the sound of my own heartbeat in my ears.

"Dammit, Steve," I think, gripping the edge of the table as my anger simmers beneath the surface. "Don't you dare lie to me."

"Whiskey," he finally says, swallowing hard, "I don't know where you're getting this information, but—"

"Whiskey, I swear to you," Steve insists, a note of desperation creeping into his voice. "I have no idea what you're talking about. I'm not involved with the Russians or the Chinese."

"Is that so?" I say, my anger rising like a tide. I can feel the heat building up in my cheeks as I try to keep my composure. I've known Steve for years, and I want to believe him, but the evidence tells a different story.

"Alright then," I continue, forcing myself to stay calm. "Let's go through this together, shall we?" With that, I begin presenting the evidence we've gathered. Photos, documents, and emails from various sources, all pointing to one undeniable conclusion: Steve Stevens has betrayed his country.

"Explain this, Steve," I demand, feeling a mix of anger and determination coursing through me. "How do you explain these emails between Russian and Chinese officials copying you?"

Steve's eyes dart back and forth between the incriminating images on the screen, his face growing paler by the second. He opens his mouth to speak, but no words come out. The silence is deafening.

"Whiskey, I–" he stammers, his voice cracking under the weight of his own guilt. "I can explain."

"Then do it, Steve!" I shout, unable to contain my fury any longer. "Explain how you could betray your country, your friends, and everything we stand for!"

My heart races as I watch him struggle to find the words, his face a portrait of shame and fear. The man I once called a friend has been replaced by a stranger, and I can't help but wonder if I ever truly knew him at all.

"Please, Whiskey," he pleads, his voice barely audible. "You have to understand..."

"Understand?" I spit back, my voice dripping with contempt. "I understand that you've made your choices, Steve. Now you have to live with the consequences."

And as the weight of Steve's betrayal sinks in, I realize that our friendship is well and truly broken, shattered by lies and treachery. No matter what comes next, one thing is certain: nothing will ever be the same again.

The air feels suffocating, thick with tension as Steve's eyes dart around the screen. Sweat beads on his forehead and pools at the base of his neck. He looks like a cornered animal, and I can't help but feel a mix of anger and pity.

"Whiskey," he stammers, fear lacing his words. "I didn't want to do it. They made me."

"Who?" I demand, gripping the edge of the table. My heart hammers against my ribs, a drumbeat echoing my fury. I need answers, and I need them now. "Who made you betray us?"

"I–" Steve hesitates for a moment, swallowing hard. "They threatened my family, Whiskey. I didn't have a choice."

"Your family?" The words come out like a knife, sharp and edged with disbelief. This man, who I once trusted with my life, has chosen blood over loyalty. But is that enough? Would I have done the same? The questions gnaw at me, making my stomach churn.

"Damn it, Steve!" I slam my fist down on the table, rattling the glass and making him jump. "You could've come to me, to anyone! We would've helped you!"

"Would you?" he shoots back, his voice wavering. "Would you really, Whiskey?"

"Of course!" I shout, feeling a vein throb in my temple. "That's what friends do! We don't sell each other out to the goddamn Russians and Chinese!"

He flinches at the accusation, but there's no denying the truth. Steve betrayed us all, and nothing he says now can change that.

"Look, I know I messed up," he says, his voice barely audible. "But you have to believe me, Whiskey. I never wanted to hurt anyone. I just wanted to protect my family."

"By selling out your country?" I scoff, shaking my head in disgust. "You've got a hell of a way of showing it, Steve."

"Please, Whiskey," he pleads, desperation seeping into his words like ink on wet parchment. "You know me. You know I'd never do this unless I had no other choice."

I stare at him, my heart heavy with the weight of our shattered friendship. He's right; I do know him. But that doesn't change what he's done.

"Choices have consequences, Steve," I say, my voice low and cold. "And you chose wrong."

I watch Steve's face closely as he gathers the courage to confess his secret. He hesitates, swallowing hard before speaking.

"Whiskey, I... I have a mistress in China," he says, his voice cracking with shame. "And we have a child together."

My jaw clenches involuntarily, but I force myself to keep listening. He owes me an explanation for all this.

"Her name is Mei," he continues, staring down at his lap. "She and our son were threatened by the Chinese government. They told me that if I didn't cooperate, they'd take my son away from her... Maybe even worse."

His voice falters, and for the first time since the call began, I see real fear in his eyes. As much as I want to hold him accountable for his actions, I can't ignore the anguish on his face.

"Steve..." My voice softens slightly, the anger subsiding just enough to allow some compassion through. "Why didn't you come to me? We could've figured something out together."

He shakes his head, tears glistening in his eyes. "You don't understand, Whiskey. They have eyes everywhere. If I told anyone, they would know. And they wouldn't hesitate to make good on their threats."

I rub my temples, trying to make sense of it all. The man I knew as a loyal friend, now exposed as a betrayer, caught in a web of international espionage. The world suddenly feels like it's spinning too fast, and I struggle to keep my balance.

"Steve, I get that you were in a tough spot," I say, trying to keep my voice steady. "But you still made the choice to betray your country. That's not something I can easily forgive."

"Whiskey, please," he begs, his desperation palpable even through the screen. "I never wanted any of this. I just wanted to protect my family."

"Family?" I spit the word out, my anger flaring up again. "What about your country, your position as head of the FBI and U.S. counterpart of the Five Eyes Alliance. An alliance that is specifically tasked with targeting Chinese Spying, Steve? What about the trust all five of the free countries place in you and each other?"

He looks away, unable to meet my gaze. "I'm sorry," he murmurs, his voice barely audible.

"Sorry doesn't cut it," I say coldly. "You made your choice, and now you have to live with the consequences."

One thing is clear: no matter how complex his situation, Steve's actions remain unforgivable. And I can't forget that.

"Please, Whiskey," Steve pleads, his voice wavering. "You gotta understand the choices I had to make." His eyes, once so full of determination, are now begging me for mercy. "I was backed into a corner. My family's lives were on the line, still are on the line."

I stare at him, my heart pounding like a freight train in my chest. The man I once called my friend stands before me, broken and desperate.

"Steve," I say, my voice steady despite the turmoil raging inside me. "We all have to make hard choices. But you crossed a line. You put our country in danger."

My hand trembles as I reach for my glass of whiskey, the amber liquid swirling like a storm within its confines. I take a sip, the burn reminding me that I'm still alive, still fighting. "You know as well as I do that there's no coming back from this," I tell him.

"Whiskey, please–" he starts, but I cut him off.

"Enough!" I growl, my anger boiling over. "I've made my decision, the information has been passed on to the White House and I stand by it. Your choices led you here, Steve, and now you gotta face the consequences."

The truth settles between us like a funeral shroud. There's no going back, no returning to the days when we stood side by side, united in our goals.

"Goodbye, Steve," I say quietly, my voice filled with regret and sorrow. "I wish things could've been different."

As I end the call and his image flashes from the screen, I'm left alone with the weight of this betrayal, the ghost of our friendship haunting the corners of my mind. But I know I made the right decision – for the sake of my country and all those who still believe in it.

"God help you, Steve," I mutter, reaching for my whiskey once more.

Chapter 14
THE CLIMAX

The salty sea breeze tickles my skin as I glance out at the sea, feeling the weight of the world on my shoulders. My seventy-two-year-old heart is pounding like a young buck's as the group and I huddle around the computer screen at my villa. It is approaching midnight in Israel, on March twenty fifth. The military operation is in full swing, and we can only wait and pray that our intel has made a difference.

Pacing back and forth across the tiled terrace. The tiny beads of sweat on my forehead feel like they're about to merge into a river.

"Whiskey, sit down," Rosa urges softly, her dark eyes filled with concern. "You're making everyone more nervous."

"Can't help it," I reply tersely, gritting my teeth. My mind races, conjuring up images of fire and destruction that could have been unleashed on the world if they fail. I can see it so clearly — the pipeline in ruins, the economies of countless countries crippled, innocent lives lost in an instant. It's enough to make me sick.

"Any news?" I bark at Bob, who's hunched over the computer, his trembling fingers hovering over the keyboard. Becca stands by his side, her hand on his shoulder, steadying him.

"Nothing yet, Whiskey," he replies, his voice barely audible.

"Damn," I mutter under my breath, resuming my pacing.

"Hey, man," Josh says, trying to inject some optimism into the tense atmosphere. "We did our part, right? Now we just gotta trust that the guys on the ground are doing theirs."

"Whiskey," Josh interjects, his calm demeanor a stark contrast to my own agitation, "we need to believe in our military and the mission."

"Look," Karlie says suddenly, her voice barely above a whisper. She points at the computer screen, her eyes wide with anticipation.

We all snap to attention, crowding around the monitor as Bob scrolls through the latest updates. The air feels heavy with expectation, our breaths collectively held as we wait for the news that could change everything.

"Come on," I breathe, my hands clenched into fists. "Come on."

Brian, Rosa, Josh, Karlie, Bob, Becca and Katya, exchange nervous glances, their eyes reflecting a mixture of fear and hope. We're quite the team, each one of us carrying secrets, scars, and ghosts from our past. But we've also come together, bound by the trust we've built in each other and in our shared mission.

"Please," I whisper, my voice cracking with emotion. "Please let it be enough."

The Climax

"Here it is!" Bob exclaims as the screen flashes with a bold message: ATTACK THWARTED. The weight of the room seems to lift in an instant, replaced by a palpable sense of relief that surges through every one of us.

"Hot damn, we did it!" I shout, my face breaking into a wide grin as I look around at my friends – no, my family – their own expressions mirroring mine. We've prevented a global crisis, together.

"Whiskey, you ol' dog," Rosa says, her voice choked with emotion. "You did it"

"No Rosa, we all did it!"

Brian chimes in, his usual stoic demeanor giving way to a hint of pride. "You led us here, Whiskey. All of us."

"Thank you," I whisper, my voice thick with gratitude. "But remember, we did this together. Now, let's celebrate!"

"Three...two...one!" We shout in unison, the countdown culminating in raucous cheers and thunderous applause. Our hearts pound like drums, a symphony of relief and victory echoing through the room.

"We really did it!" exclaims Brian.

"Yessir, we sure as hell did," I grin, my chest swelling with pride. I look around at my friends, their faces beaming back at me, and I know that our bond is strong and forever.

The gravity of what's just happened settling on my shoulders. My hands tremble as I reach for my ringing phone, excitement coursing through my veins like an electric current. "It's the White House", I take a deep breath, preparing myself for the conversation ahead.

My hand trembles as I hold the phone, each ring echoing through the room like the beat of a war drum. My friends watch me with bated breath, their eyes wide with anticipation and anxiety.

"Hello?" I answer, my voice steady despite the pounding in my chest.

"This is your President," the voice on the other end replies, sending a shiver down my spine. "Who am I speaking with?"

"Mr. President, this is Whiskey Black," I say, taking a deep breath to gather my thoughts.

"Whisky, we've thwarted an imminent attack on a major oil pipeline in Israel, thanks to the solid intel from you and your team. The attackers were intercepted just in time," the President says, his voice filled with admiration. "You've saved countless lives and prevented a potential global crisis."

"How did you do it, how did you gather the intel, tell me everything," he urges, his voice firm yet attentive.

"Over the past several weeks, my team and I have been working to uncover a network of spies and double agents within various governments and corporations," I continue, my heart racing as I recount our dangerous exploits.

"Your teamwork is truly inspiring," the President says, and I can hear the smile in his voice. "Please pass on my gratitude to each and every one of them. Their actions will not be forgotten."

"Thank you, sir," I reply, feeling my chest tighten with pride. My gaze sweeps across the faces of my friends – Brian, Rosa, Josh, Karlie, Bob, Becca, and Katya - all of whom had played their part in this incredible mission. I swallow hard, fighting back emotion. "It's been an honor to work alongside such a dedicated group of people, and I know we wouldn't have succeeded without everyone's unique skills and unwavering devotion.

"About Steve Stevens?" I ask.

"I can't talk about specifics but it appears as though Steve Stevens committed suicide earlier today. An unfortunate situation all around. I'd like to ask you and your team to keep all intel and details of your work and this mission classified. I will be sending officials to debrief you and your team in the coming days. Will that work for you?"

"Yes sir, not a problem."

Your country owes you a debt of gratitude. God speed Whiskey."

The line goes dead, and I find myself staring at the phone in my hand, the words of the President still ringing in my ears. Shock and awe ripple through me, a tide pulling me under as the reality of what we've done washes over me. We stopped them – stopped a global catastrophe that would've changed the world as we know it. Steve Stevens, I ponder for a moment, "his sudden suicide is very convenient for the administration or did I push him too far? I'll never know."

"Guys," I say, turning to face my friends with a smile, "the President sends his personal thanks."

A chorus of cheers erupts around me, as we revel in our victory.

"Let's celebrate," Karlie suggests, grabbing a bottle of champagne from the counter. "This calls for a toast."

"Here, here!" Brian agrees, clapping his hands together, and the rest chime in as well.

Chapter 15
LOOSE ENDS

The sun fades, and the breeze is nice on La Sirena rooftop, where we're all gathered. I take a swig of my beer and look at my friends - Brian, Rosa, Josh, Karlie, Bob, and Becca - each lost in their own thoughts, nursing their drinks. The mission is over, but it's left us with a few scars.

"Alright," I say, "we've got some loose ends to tie up."

Brian nods, his blue eyes scanning the group. "First off, we need to make sure no one can trace anything back to us. I doubt anyone will, but better safe than sorry. Bob, Becca, can you double-check the encryption on our devices and erase all trace of our communications?

"Not a problem," says Bob. He has begun struggling with early signs of dementia, but he's still sharp when it comes to technology. Becca, ever supportive, is always there to help him through the rough patches.

"Rosa and I will handle any remaining connections we have on the ground," Brian continues, glancing at his wife. The loyalty between those two runs deep, and I know they'd do anything for each other.

I can't help but reflect on everything that's happened. We've been through hell and back, but in the end, it's only made our bond stronger. I look at each of my friends - Brian, the jack-of-all-trades; Rosa, the fiercely loyal wife; Josh, the strategic thinker; Karlie, the cunning journalist turned free-spirited artist; Bob, the determined tech wizard; and Becca, the patient ingenious hacker.

"You know how much you mean to me, right?" I ask, my voice cracking slightly. They all look at me, their expressions softening.

"Of course we do, Whiskey," says Becca warmly. "We wouldn't be here if it weren't for you."

"That's right," adds Bob, raising his beer in a toast. "To Whiskey, the glue that holds us all together."

~

Just as we're about to disperse, Agent Santiago and her team emerge from the stairwell. Their return signals the end of their escort mission; they've successfully seen Katya out of Mexico. I can see the weariness etched on their faces, but there's also a sense of pride in their eyes.

"Whiskey," Agent Santiago greets me with a nod. "We just got back from taking Ms. Rublev to a secure location."

"Thank you, Agent Santiago," I say sincerely. "I know it wasn't an easy task, but your team handled it with professionalism and dedication."

"Your gratitude is appreciated, Whiskey," she replies, brushing off my praise modestly. "Our job was made easier by your resourcefulness."

My friends chime in, expressing their thanks to Agent Santiago and her team. We all understand the gravity of what we've accomplished and the importance of the support we received. It's not every day that a group of retired expats gets involved in international espionage, but somehow, we managed to pull through.

"Before we leave," Agent Santiago says, addressing our group, "we want to ensure you that everything we were involved in here remains classified.

"Thank you," I reply, feeling a weight lift off my shoulders. With the assurance of our safety, we can finally move on from this chapter and return to our lives in Puerto Morelos.

"Lastly," she says, her eyes meeting mine, "we'll continue monitoring Ms. Rublev's situation. We believe she's genuine about wanting a fresh start, but we'll keep an eye on her, just in case."

"Much appreciated, Agent Santiago," I say, my heart aching as I think about Katya. Despite everything, I hope she finds the new life she seeks.

~

Just another sunny day at Dive Bar, as me and my friends gather around a weathered wooden table, cold beers in hand. The salty breeze, carrying with it the laughter of locals and tourists alike. It's good to be back.

"Who would've thought that a bunch of retired expats could pull off a mission like that?" Becca muses, a playful glint in her eyes. "We must've learned a thing or two from those old spy movies."

"Or maybe it was just luck," Karlie chimes in, smiling. "Either way, I'm glad we're back here on the beach."

"Agreed," Josh adds, grinning broadly. "Now, who's up for some bocce ball?"

"Count me in," Bob says, downing the last of his beer. Becca nods enthusiastically in agreement.

As we get up to play, I can't help but feel a sense of contentment wash over me. These people, once strangers, have become my family, bound together by our experiences. We may have stumbled into international espionage, but our friendship has emerged stronger.

"Hey Whiskey!" Brian calls out, tossing me a bocce ball. "You gonna show us how it's done?"

My competitive spirit kicks in, and I accept the challenge with a grin. "You bet."

After several rounds of friendly competition, laughter, and good-natured banter, I decide to take a walk along the beach, the sand warm beneath my feet. The familiar sights and sounds of Puerto Morelos embrace me like an old friend – the turquoise waves lapping at the shore, the distant call of seagulls, the hum of conversation from nearby beach bars.

I let my thoughts wander, reflecting on all that's happened and the bonds we've formed. Our lives have been irrevocably changed, but my friends and I have weathered it together. I find solace in the simple beauty of this place. It's a comforting reminder that amidst the chaos of the world, there are still pockets of paradise one can escape.

As I stroll along the water's edge, the waves lapping at my feet. My mind drifts to Katya, her enigmatic smile and the secrets she'd hidden behind it. Our time together had been short but intense, stirring emotions in me I hadn't felt in years. I can't help but wonder where she is now.

Just then, my phone vibrates in my pocket, startling me from my thoughts. I glance at the screen, seeing an unknown number flashing across it. A slight unease settles in my chest, but I answer the call anyway.

"Hello?"

"Whiskey," a familiar voice murmurs, sending a shiver down my spine. "It's Katya."

"Katya?" I pause for a moment, emotions swirling inside me like a storm. "I didn't expect to hear from you."

"I wanted to thank you," she says softly. "You and your friends risked so much to help me, and I owe you all a debt I can never repay."

"Where are you?" I ask, my voice betraying the concern I can't quite shake off. "It sounds like you are near the ocean."

"Somewhere safe," she replies evasively. "Starting a new life."

"Are you happy?" The question slips out before I can stop it, revealing more vulnerability than I'd like to admit.

"Whiskey, our relationship was... complicated," she admits, hesitating for a moment. "But yes, I am happy. And I want you to be too."

"Complicated is an understatement," I chuckle, the sound tinged with sadness. "But I'm glad you're safe, Katya."

"Take care of yourself, Whiskey," she whispers, her voice heavy with emotion. "I will never forget you."

Just then I hear someone in the background speaking a foreign language. "Is that...?"

The line goes dead, leaving me standing on the beach with the finality of her words ringing in my ears. I look out at the ocean, its endless expanse stretching before me like a promise. Katya's presence had challenged me, forced me to do the impossible.

"Was that Greek I heard," I murmur to the waves, "ah, it's all Greek to me," I chuckle to myself.

"Hey, Whiskey!" a voice calls out from behind me.

I turn, catching sight of Brian jogging towards me, his face flushed from exertion. He glances at the phone in my hand, then back up at me with a knowing expression. "You're still thinking about her, huh?"

"Can't help it," I admit, my gaze drifting back out to the sea. "She changed my life."

"She sure did," he agrees, wiping a bead of sweat from his brow. "But you know what? We got through it, and now we're stronger for it."

"Sometimes it's hard to see that silver lining," I reply, my mind still clouded by memories of Katya. My heart aches with the weight of her absence, I can't deny the impact she had on me.

"Look around you, Whiskey. This place is paradise. And we've got each other — a crew of expats who somehow found each other in this crazy world." Brian grins, slapping me on the back. "You can't ask for much more than that."

"Maybe you're right," I concede, a smile tugging at the corners of my lips. "Maybe I just needed a reminder."

"Come on," Brian urges, nodding towards a group of our friends gathered further down the beach. "Let's go join the others."

As we walk side by side, I take in the familiar sights and sounds that define my everyday life in Puerto Morelos. The laughter of children playing in the surf, and the gentle rustle of palm trees swaying in the breeze — these are the things I've come to know and love.

"Hey, Whiskey," Rosa calls out as we approach the group, a smile lighting up her face. "We were just talking about planning a bocce ball tournament for next weekend. You in?"

"Sure thing," I reply, feeling the warmth of their camaraderie. "Wouldn't miss it for the world."

As we gather together, sharing stories and laughter, I can't help but feel a sense of hope and possibility wash over me. Yes, the world is a chaotic place, filled with uncertainty and danger. But here, in this slice of paradise, I've found something worth fighting for — a family forged not by blood, but by trust and shared experiences.

Just then, a seductive voice with a French accent reaches my ear from behind. "Mimosa por favor?"

I slide on the empty stool next to the beautiful brunette. "Hello there Mimosa, I'm Whiskey."

She turns her head slowly and gives me a disdainful look. She rolls her eyes and snorts. "Go away, before I throw my drink on your face." She waves her hand dismissively and turns back to the bar, ignoring me completely.

"She's not a spy sent to target me, that much is clear," I chuckle to myself.

Made in the USA
Columbia, SC
09 December 2023

27427534R00076